Destination
Wedding

A Novel

Deanna Lynn Sletten

Destination Wedding

Copyright 2014 © Deanna Lynn Sletten

ISBN-10:1941212131
ISBN-13:978-1-941212-13-4

Editor: Denise Vitola
Cover Designer: Deborah Bradseth of Tugboat Design

Excerpt from Walking Sam Copyright 2016 © Deanna Lynn Sletten

Destination
Wedding

A Novel

Chapter One

Claire Martin discreetly glanced at her watch with one eye as she watched her customer with the other turn this way and that in front of the three-way mirror. Claire had to be out of the shop in five minutes or else she'd be late meeting with her daughter, and she didn't want to be late. Today was important.

Claire smiled and nodded at the woman in front of her, agreeing that the long-waisted sweater did make her look thinner and the dark, skinny jeans were perfect with it. Claire didn't want to be rude. After all, this lady was a regular customer at Claire's clothing store, the Belle Boutique, and regular customers were important for business. But she did wish the woman would hurry up and pick an outfit.

Claire absently pushed a stray strand of her sandy blond hair behind her ear and then began twirling the charm bracelet on her wrist round and round. She glanced at herself in the floor-to-ceiling mirror to check her appearance. Her hair was still neatly in place and her makeup still fresh looking. She plucked off a stray strand of string that had somehow come to rest on her sleeve. Perfect.

Finally, the customer decided that she loved the outfit she had on, and Claire politely excused herself and said that Ariana would ring up her purchases.

Claire rushed to the back room and into her office, slipped off her pumps, and pulled on a pair of knee-high, leather boots over her leggings. Today, she was dressed warmly despite the fact that it should already be spring outside. Unfortunately, spring in Minnesota could come as early as March or as late as May, and this year it chose the latter. Wearing a sweater dress and leggings in April seemed ridiculous, but not when the temperature was in the forties outside and snow was still on the ground. Grabbing her red, wool coat off the back of the office chair, Claire walked swiftly through the store and up to the front counter where her Assistant Manager, Ariana Flores, stood behind the register.

"Did she buy the sweater and jeans?" Claire asked, noting that the customer was no longer in the store.

"Yes. And the dress and brown trousers, too. I rounded it all up nicely with a set of bangle bracelets and earrings," Ariana said.

Claire smiled at Ariana as she slipped on her coat. Ariana had been working for her for almost five years and Claire didn't know what she'd do without her. Ariana was in her mid-forties, just as Claire was, but where Claire was tall with light skin, hair, and eyes, Ariana was the exact opposite. Ariana's Hispanic heritage shined through with a golden-brown complexion, big, brown eyes, and straight black hair that she usually put up in a twist. She was shorter than Claire, which she made up for by wearing very high heels. And Ariana always dressed with a vibrant style, showing off the clothes they sold in the most flattering way. Most of all, though, Ariana was loyal and a good friend who sometimes teased the very serious Claire mercilessly when she felt like it.

"Wonderful," Claire said. "I should hand all my customers over to you so you can add accessories to their purchases."

Ariana shrugged. "It's what we do. By the way, Steven-not-Steve called again to remind you that you are having dinner with him tonight."

Claire held back the chuckle that threatened to escape her

lips. Steven Sievers, the man she was dating, did not like being called Steve, and had bluntly reminded Ariana of that the one time she called him Steve. Ever since then, Ariana referred to him as Steven-not-Steve.

"Why in the world does he think I'll forget? I've never forgotten before."

Ariana waggled her eyebrows. "Maybe he doesn't want you to forget because he's hoping for a little nookie tonight."

Claire rolled her eyes. "You've been reading too many of those Fifty Shades type books. They're tarnishing your good sense."

Ariana laughed. "You'd better go or your daughter will be angry with you."

Claire waved goodbye and hurried out the door into the dreary, gray day. She picked her way across the parking lot that separated the strip mall where her boutique was located from another long strip of shops. Claire's boutique was just one of many in the Ann Arbor Shopping Center in the town of Maple Grove. Everything from clothing, jewelry, and shoe stores to pet supplies and craft stores filled the strategically arranged buildings with restaurants and hotels sprinkled here and there. It was a busy place to say the least, and the perfect spot for Claire's business.

The parking lot was splattered with muddy, mushy snow that was melting away and leaving dirty puddles in its wake. Claire stopped at the busy intersection that separated one shopping area from another and waited for the traffic signal to change so she could cross. She pulled her coat tightly around her against the chilly breeze. One thing was for certain, she was looking forward to leaving town for a week and getting away from this awful weather.

After crossing the intersection, Claire walked down another strip of shops until she came to her destination.

Stepping inside Marissa's Bridal Shop, Claire almost ran into her daughter, Amanda, and her daughter's best friend, Kaylie Thompson, in the entryway.

"Am I late, Mandy?" Claire asked, out of breath from her trek across the shopping compound.

Mandy shook her head, her hair swishing back and forth from the movement. "No, we just got here."

Claire hugged both Mandy and Kaylie in turn. The girls had been best friends since middle school, and Claire felt like a second mother to Kaylie. The two girls were the exact opposites in size and looks. While Mandy was tall and lean with chestnut brown hair cut into a sensible bob and had dark blue eyes, Kaylie was shorter and petite with long, straight, blond hair and light blue eyes. But their personalities had always meshed well and they had been the best of friends for so long that they might as well have been sisters.

Claire looked around the bridal boutique with raised brows. "Is it just us or will Janice be joining us?" she asked Mandy. Janice Fisher was Mandy's soon to be mother-in-law.

"Janice said she'd rather be pleasantly surprised on the day of the wedding," Mandy replied with a sarcastic emphasis on the word *pleasantly*. She shrugged. "So, yes, it's just us."

Claire nodded, but what she really wanted to do was say something scathing about Janice. She held her tongue instead. While Mandy might have to occasionally put up with her in-laws at family events, she wasn't marrying them. Mandy was marrying Craig, and he was a wonderful young man. Trying to sound generous, Claire offered, "I suppose it isn't as much fun being the mother of the groom instead of the bride. She probably feels left out no matter how many things we invite her to. Don't give it much thought."

Mandy nodded. Just then the owner of the shop, Marissa, came swooping down upon them in a whirl of energy, gave hugs all around, and then led the small group to the mirrored dressing rooms so Mandy and Kaylie could try on their dresses.

Kaylie went first so they could save the most anticipated dress for last. The strapless, aquamarine, short satin dress she'd chosen fit her to a tee and was the perfect color for a beach wedding. After the three women exclaimed admiration for the dress, it was Mandy's turn to try on her wedding gown. Marissa went in the room with Mandy to help her slip into the dress while Claire and Kaylie waited excitedly out in the mirrored display area.

Finally, Marissa came out through the curtain with a grin on her face and her hands clasped tightly in front of her as if in silent applause. "Here she is," Marissa announced. "The future Mrs. Craig Fisher."

Mandy swept through the curtain in a vision of satin, lace, and ruffles amidst gasps from Claire and Kaylie. She glided over to the pedestal in front of the three-way mirror and stepped up on it, then turned to face her mother with a small smile on her face.

Claire stood with her hands over her mouth, taken aback at the sight of the lovely princess standing before her. She had seen the dress on Mandy countless times, before alterations and without the veil and shoes. But today, with the entire ensemble on, her Mandy, her little girl now grown up, was a beautiful sight to behold.

"Well, Mom? What do you think?" Mandy asked.

"It's absolutely breathtaking," Claire said. "It's just… perfect." And it was. Mandy had chosen a gown that was both simple, yet elegant, and that suited her no-nonsense personality. It was a creamy white strapless dress fitted at the bust and waist then billowing out to a full skirt with a small, flowing train. The skirt was made up of layers of short ruffles which gave it a frothy look, like the foam on the ocean as the waves hit the beach. The veil hung over Mandy's bare shoulders and was trimmed in a delicate application of beads. It was a sophisticated, beautiful gown and was perfect for a ceremony on a sandy beach—Mandy's dream wedding. Looking at her normally serious daughter dressed like an angel in white, Claire suddenly wondered where the years had gone. Twenty-four years. Years of smiles, laughter, and tears. Years of baby dolls, trikes, kissing booboos, and starting Kindergarten. Those years had morphed into prom dresses, shaggy boyfriends, and college dorm rooms. A first apartment, a first job, and then engagement. And now, after everything, marriage. Time had passed too quickly.

"It's gorgeous!" Kaylie exclaimed after she finally found her voice. "You look like a princess."

Mandy smiled at Kaylie, and then her mother. "This is it," she said. "In three days we'll be off to the Caribbean and within the week, I'll be married. It's incredible, isn't it?"

Claire nodded, afraid to speak in case she choked on the tears she was holding back.

"I can't wait until Dad sees my dress. Won't he be surprised?" Mandy asked.

All the delightful memories that had been embracing Claire that very moment dropped to the floor at the mention of Mandy's father. Claire had been actively trying to forget that one detail—Jim, and his new, younger wife, would be at the wedding, too.

* * *

The wedding gown was carefully bagged as was Kaylie's dress and all the accessories. Claire paid the balance along with buying all the extras like a box to store the dress in after the wedding. The three women waved goodbye to Marissa and walked out into the gloomy day in the fading, late afternoon light.

Kaylie hugged Claire and Mandy goodbye and ran off to her little sports car, carefully avoiding the larger of the muddy puddles in the parking lot. Claire helped Mandy to her car where they carefully hung the bagged gown on the hook in the back seat and laid out all the other purchases.

"So, have you heard from your father lately?" Claire asked, trying to sound indifferent, but failing miserably. *Please say he isn't coming and bringing that annoying wife of his. Please, please, please.*

Mandy stared at her mother a moment before answering. "I just talked to him this morning. And yes, he's still planning on coming, Mom. Dad wouldn't miss my wedding day." Mandy threw her mother a sly grin. "Remember, I can read your mind."

Claire had the good grace to look sheepish. Jim wouldn't miss his daughter's wedding, she knew that better than anyone. But it didn't stop Claire from wishing she didn't have to spend an entire week on an island with her ex-husband and the woman he'd left her for.

Mandy leaned forward and pulled Claire into a hug. "I know this isn't going to be easy, Mom, but I couldn't get married without both of you there. Please, for my sake, try to make it work?"

Claire hugged her daughter tightly before slowly pulling away. "Of course, I'll make it work. I'm always polite to him and that woman. I didn't say one mean thing to her or him at the engagement party, remember?" *I wanted to spill red wine all over her skimpy, tight yellow dress, but I refrained.*

Mandy rewarded Claire with one of her serious stares, the kind that reminded Claire so much of her ex-husband. Mandy had Jim's thick, wavy, chestnut brown hair and his deep blue eyes, a lethal combination that attracted people easily. But where her father had an outgoing, easy nature about him, always ready with a rakish grin, Mandy was more serious and reserved, like her mother. Yet, Claire couldn't help but always be reminded of Jim every time she looked at her daughter.

"Mom, that *woman* has a name. It's Diane. And I know you're trying. It's just for a week. I promise you will barely even see them while we're there."

Claire nodded, realizing that this was probably true. After all, even though it was a small island, there were plenty of places she could be that he wasn't. And miles of beach. She looked forward to walking a lot on the warm beaches and enjoying the sun and ocean breezes.

"It's too bad Steven isn't coming with you," Mandy said, interrupting Claire's thoughts. "You're going to be the only person there who isn't part of a couple."

Claire bit her lip. Yes, it would have been nice to have had someone along to share the romantic trip with, but she wasn't going to let that ruin her good time. There were plenty of other people she loved coming along like her brother, Glen, and sister-in-law, Lisa, Kaylie, the best man's wife Angela, and of course Mandy. Claire would have plenty of fun enjoying the entire wedding party despite Jim being there.

"Earth to Mom," Mandy said, waving her hand in front of Claire's face.

Claire snapped out of her stupor. "Sorry. I was just thinking how much fun we'll all have on the island, even though Steven won't be along." She looked at her watch. "Speaking of which, I'd better get going or I'll be late. I'm meeting Steven for dinner tonight and I have to go back to the shop first, then home to change."

Mandy drove Claire over to the boutique and they hugged goodbye. The next time they'd see each other would be at the airport on Monday. They both had plenty to do before taking off for an entire week.

Chapter Two

James Martin sat on the crowded commuter flight from Minneapolis to Chicago, still fuming at his boss for making him take this trip. It was late Friday afternoon, and instead of being on a plane he should be heading home to pack and get ready for his flight on Monday to Paradise for his daughter's wedding.

Earlier in the day, when his boss had told him there were problems needing his expertise in the Chicago offices of the office supply company he worked for, Jim couldn't believe his ears. His boss knew Jim was heading off for a week to the Bahamas for his daughter's wedding. Jim didn't really dare to say no, though. He'd been working at this company since before college graduation, but he knew that no job in this economy was safe. If his boss thought he was capable of fixing problems in Chicago, then he'd better go. He wasn't happy about it, that was for certain.

Jim ran his hand through his hair and down the back of his neck. The flight hadn't even taken off yet and he was already tired of sitting. He was tense, stressed, and downright mad. Now, instead of leaving from home with the rest of the wedding party on Monday morning, he'd be flying out of Chicago. He hoped he'd packed everything he needed for the Bahamas. He hoped Mandy wouldn't be upset with him for having to change his flight. Ugg, life was complicated.

Jim's cell phone buzzed in his pocket and he winced when

he saw who it was, but he answered it because he knew she would continue calling until he did.

"Hello, Diane."

"Where are you?"

"I'm fine. How are you?" Jim said, sarcastically.

"I don't care how you are, I asked you where you were," Diane's voice screeched over the phone.

Jim sighed. "I'm on a flight to Chicago for the weekend. The boss wanted me to straighten out a few problems in that location. If you had just asked around the office, you'd know where I was."

"I'm not going to ask random people in our office where my soon-to-be ex-husband is," Diane hissed through the line. "You promised me we'd go through the divorce papers before you left for the wedding. I want to get this over with."

No one wanted to get this marriage over with faster than Jim. "I'm sorry, but there's nothing I can do. We'll talk about this when I get back." When he heard no response, Jim figured she'd hung up on him. He pictured her angrily slamming down the receiver as if it had been an old land-line phone. Lucky for him, all she could do was push a button to cut off the call.

The flight attendant walked by slowly checking to make sure everyone was belted in before take-off. She smiled down at Jim through glossy, red lips and winked one expertly painted eye. Jim rolled his eyes. The woman was young and lovely, and had been flirting with him since he boarded. This happened to him a lot. Even at the age of forty-six, he maintained himself well with workouts several times a week and there was only a hint of grey highlighting his hair. But he wasn't interested. He'd already made that mistake once, going after a younger woman. Now that younger woman was making his life a living hell. He certainly wasn't going to make that mistake again.

Jim rested his head on the back of his seat and closed his

eyes, trying to block out his surroundings. He forced himself to think of sugar sand beaches that stretched on for miles, blue-green water foaming white, and an icy Piña Colada in his hand. Instead, his mind wandered to the blond hair, blue eyes, and soft oval face of his first wife, Claire. His college sweetheart, his wife of twenty years, and the mother of his only child. He wondered how she was handling the last-minute stresses of the wedding. He hadn't seen her since the engagement party last fall, and had only spoken to her once since then to set the budget for the wedding. Even though Jim had said he'd cover the entire expense, Claire had refused to drop the whole bill on him. She was stubborn, self-sufficient, and proud, and had insisted on paying for a portion of their daughter's wedding. For some strange reason, Jim had found that appealing. No matter what had transpired between them four years ago when he'd left her for Diane, she'd still held her own and taken care of herself. He wished Diane had turned out to be half the woman Claire was.

Jim wondered if Claire still hated him for leaving her. She'd always been polite when they had to be together, although it was a stilted form of politeness. She'd never made a scene when Diane was around, either. Maybe, just maybe, he'd be able to return to her good graces during their vacation on the island. It would be nice to be, if nothing else, at least friends again.

Jim's eyes suddenly popped open when he remembered about Steven, the man Claire had been dating for the past two years. Steven Sievers, real estate broker and owner of a branch of Century 21 Real Estate. Stiff, stuck-up, stick-up-his-ass Steven. Jim couldn't stand the guy, much less understand what Claire saw in him.

As the plane finally took off for O'Hare International Airport in Chicago, Jim pushed aside all thoughts of Diane,

Steven, and even his boss and concentrated on looking forward to Monday and moonlit nights on sandy beaches with the peaceful sound of ocean waves breaking against the shore.

* * *

Claire sat across from Steven in a cozy booth in the back corner of the eloquent steak and seafood restaurant. The lights in the room were muted and candles illuminated the tables. The setting felt intimate and private, like they were nestled in a cocoon away from the rest of the world.

In the two years they'd been dating, Claire only remembered coming to this restaurant once before. It had been on their first date, and at the time, Claire had assumed Steven was trying to impress her with the fancy decor and high prices. Tonight, however, she was confused. It wasn't her birthday and it wasn't Valentine's Day, the only two instances she could think of when he would go out of his way to bring her here. She watched Steven intently as the waiter poured their wine, wondering what he was thinking and why they were at this particular restaurant tonight.

Claire watched as Steven tasted the wine, nodded to the waiter, and then turned his smile toward her. Steven was a handsome man in his own way. He was tall, over six foot, and lean, although maybe a tad too thin by some standards. His dark blond hair was always kept short and neat, and while his hazel eyes rarely sparkled with delight, or for any other reason, they were kind. Steven didn't have the easy nature or cavalier grin that came so easily to her ex-husband, and that was fine. Claire didn't mind the fact that women didn't look twice at Steven. In fact, she was relieved they didn't. She'd already been married to a man who turned heads for years, probably still did, so it was a relief to not have to worry about that with Steven.

While some might say that Steven was rather stiff and unemotional, she thought of him more as stable, hardworking, and dependable. Stable and dependable sounded good to Claire.

"So, how was the dress fitting today?" Steven asked, bringing Claire out of her thoughts.

Claire liked the fact that Steven listened to her and always asked about her day. Some would say it was the salesman in him that made him remember details, but Claire chose to believe he was a thoughtful person instead.

"The fitting went beautifully. Mandy looked like a dream. It's going to be a fairytale wedding."

"Of course, it will. Everything you touch is done to perfection."

Claire smiled and took a sip of her wine. "Thank you. I only wish you were coming along. The island is so beautiful, and it would be a lovely romantic getaway."

Steven nodded, and looked at Claire seriously. "It would be nice, but spring is such a busy time of the year for real estate sales. Plus," he paused. "This is more of a family event, and I think it will be better for you to be there with your family without me distracting you."

Claire hesitated before she replied. She'd tried numerous times to argue the point with him that he was considered a part of the family since they'd been dating for so long. Mandy would have been happy for Steven to come along. But Steven didn't argue. He could calmly talk circles around you, but he'd never get into a heated or emotional discussion. He had his own ideas about certain things and he stuck to them.

"Still, it would have been nice. You are considered family, too," Claire said quietly.

Instead of brushing this off, Steven surprised her by taking her hand and looking deeply into her eyes. "I'm pleased you think of me that way because I'd like to become a part of your family very soon." He reached into his sports coat pocket and pulled out a small, red velvet box, opened it, and placed it on the table between them. "Claire. Will you marry me?"

Claire's eyes grew wide and her hand rose up to her throat. She stared at the simple, one-caret solitaire diamond set in a white gold band which had tiny diamonds encased in it. She swallowed hard, blinked, then looked up at Steven to see if he was serious. He was.

"Marry me, Claire," he said, smiling at her, seeming to enjoy her complete surprise.

Claire grabbed her wrist where her charm bracelet usually hung, then remembered she'd taken it off tonight. She grasped her other wrist where her watch sat, and began twirling it around and around. *Marriage? Was this for real? Was he serious?*

"I…I can't believe this," she said, finally finding her voice. "I'd have never suspected this in a million years."

Steven reached over and took the ring out of the box. He reached for Claire's hand and slipped it onto her ring finger. It fit perfectly. "Please say you'll marry me, Claire. I know you have your reservations about marrying again, but I think we'd make a good couple. We are so much alike, and we both have no illusions about love and marriage. We can make each other happy as we grow old. Marry me, Claire."

Claire stared down at the ring around her finger. She couldn't breathe. The intimate area around her lost its appeal and suddenly felt claustrophobic. Marriage, a second time around, scared the living bejeezus out of her, and she wasn't sure if she could choke out an answer, be it yes or no.

Steven sat back in his chair and stared at Claire. "You're scaring me, Claire. Just breathe. It's okay," he said calmly.

Claire closed her eyes and took a deep breath. She exhaled, letting out all the fear she'd let build up inside her. When she opened her eyes, she felt better, but the ring still felt heavy on her finger. Too heavy. Almost like a block of cement meant to drown her in a body of water.

Finally, she found her senses and her voice. "It's very beautiful, Steven," Claire said, trying to smile up at him. "It's perfect, actually. And you certainly surprised me. I had no idea you were going to propose."

Steven smiled proudly, sitting forward in his chair again.

"But I never pictured myself getting married again. I can't even imagine it. I'm sorry."

Steven's expression deflated a little, but he didn't give up. "I know we've talked about this before and you said you thought you'd never marry again. But our marriage would be different from your first. We're both older, we're both sensible, and I have no designs on leaving you for a younger woman. I think we'd make a good partnership. We each can fill in what the other person is lacking. We'd be the perfect match."

Claire sat there, allowing Steven's words to wash over her. *A good partnership. The perfect match. But what about love? What about passion?* He'd managed to propose to her, and lay out his life plan with her without ever using the word *love.*

"This is just all so sudden…"Claire began, not sure where she was headed. But Steven interrupted her.

"I know. I realize that it is. And the timing isn't perfect, I understand. I know how preoccupied you are with the upcoming trip and wedding. I only wanted you to know my intentions before you left for the Bahamas. I wanted you to know how I feel, and that I want our relationship to continue to grow. I'm serious about us, Claire, and I need you to know that."

Claire looked down at the ring still strangling her finger. She had the terrible urge to shake it off. But why? Steven was a good man. He was hardworking and stable. What was it about this ring that made her feel like she was wearing a noose?

"I just need some time to think about it, Steven," she finally said. "You're right. I do have a lot on my mind with my daughter's wedding and the trip. And this was such a surprise. Would it hurt your feelings terribly if I think it over?"

Steven smiled sweetly at her. "No, it won't hurt my feelings. I knew going into this that there was the possibility you might say no, so the fact that you want to think about it gives me hope. Take all the time you need. I know you'll make the right decision."

Claire wondered if he thought the *right decision* meant the best decision for her, or for him?

She started to slip the ring off her finger to hand it back to Steven, but he shook his head.

"Wear it awhile. Get used to feeling it on your finger. Hopefully, the ring will help you make your decision." Steven picked up the velvet ring box from the table, closed it, and handed it to Claire. She wasn't sure what to do, so she left the ring on throughout dinner to make Steven happy, but all the while she wondered, did it make her happy, too?

Much later, as Claire lay in her bed beside a soundly sleeping Steven, she picked up her left hand and looked at the ring glinting in the darkness. After bringing Claire home, Steven had asked to stay and made love to her as a way to celebrate the marriage proposal that he was sure she was going to eventually accept. Their lovemaking was nice, always had been, but it lacked the spark, warmth, and passion that Claire would have liked to feel. Or maybe it lacked a deep love commitment. Did Claire actually love Steven? Did she love him enough to promise to spend the rest of her life with him? Or was love even necessary at their ages when stability and honesty were much more important? She didn't know.

Love, passion, and a deep connection were all things that

Claire had already experienced in her married life the first time around, and where did that get her? She'd ended up alone when that passion had faded and Jim had left her. Maybe love and butterflies in the stomach and passion was overrated. Maybe what she had with Steven was mature and realistic. Maybe, just maybe, when she returned from her daughter's wedding in the Bahamas, she'd be ready to say yes.

Chapter Three

Monday morning found Claire in a state of panic as she arrived at the Minneapolis-St. Paul International Airport by cab. It was only six o'clock a.m. and the airport was quiet, the first flights of the day just starting to take off. As Claire stepped out of the cab and retrieved her carry-on bag and suitcase from the driver, she prayed she'd packed everything she needed. If she hadn't, it was too late now.

Claire stepped through the automatic doors and began looking around for the others in her group. When her eyes fell upon her soon-to-be son-in-law, Craig, one of the tallest in the group, she sighed with relief, and headed over their way.

Soon, the entire group was gathered together and the checking of the bags commenced. Each person was bringing a carry-on with their wedding clothes in it so if their luggage was lost, at least the wedding would go off without a hitch. Somehow, Mandy had stuffed her beautiful wedding gown into her small carry-on, and Claire hoped and prayed it would make the flight with as few wrinkles as possible.

It wasn't until after everyone had checked their larger bags that Claire had a chance to look around at their group and assess who was there. She knew Mandy and Craig were here, then there was Craig's parents, Janice and Carl, standing stiffly at the edge of the group. Kaylie and her boyfriend, Mark Carlson, and the best man Cameron Anderson and his wife Angela were all standing with Mandy and Craig. There were nine of them in all, counting Claire.

Claire frowned. She had been dreading seeing Jim and his wife, but as she looked around, she noted that they were missing from the group. She hurried over to Mandy and pulled her aside.

"Have you seen your father?" Claire asked. "He isn't here yet."

"Oh, with all that was going on I forgot to tell you," Mandy said. "I got a call from Dad on Saturday. He was in Chicago for work and he had to change his flight. He's flying out of Chicago this morning and meeting us in Miami."

"Oh. Diane, too?" Claire asked.

Mandy nodded. "I'm guessing she's with him. He didn't say otherwise and he didn't say we should expect her here."

As the group headed over to go through security, Claire let out a sigh of relief. At least she wouldn't have to sit and watch Jim and Diane throughout the three-and-a-half-hour flight to Miami being all lovey-dovey and cuddly. The thought of it made her stomach sick.

Everything went smoothly and the group landed in Miami on time. Once there, though, they had to run, quite literally, to catch the small plane to Marsh Harbour on the Great Abaco Island in the Bahamas. There, they met up with Claire's brother and sister-in-law, Glen and Lisa Goodwin, who'd just flown to Miami from San Diego.

"Uncle Glen! Aunt Lisa!" Mandy called with delight when she saw them at the gate. "I'm so happy you're coming along."

Glen smiled as he hugged his niece. "I wouldn't miss my only niece's wedding. You know that." He winked over to Claire. "Especially when it's in the Bahamas."

Hugs and introductions were dispersed all around and then they were hurried outside on the tarmac to board the tiny plane. Again, Claire hadn't seen Jim or Diane. Maybe his plane from

Chicago was late. Maybe they'd have to come on a later flight to the Bahamas. Claire secretly hoped so.

The group squeezed down the tiny aisle of the plane and found their seats. All the carry-ons were given to the attendant since there were no overhead compartments. Claire was the only person in the group who had to sit with a stranger since everyone else had come in pairs. Mandy and Craig sat in the seats in front of her, Glen and Lisa were behind her, and Kaylie and Mark where across the aisle from her. An elderly gentleman with a white beard and wearing tropical colored clothing sat in the window seat beside Claire. She smiled over at him when she sat down.

Mandy was just taking her seat when Claire saw her smile and wave at someone at the back of the plane.

"Dad made it," Mandy said to Claire. "He's in the back."

Claire forced herself not to turn around and look.

The flight took off and everyone settled in. The aisle was too narrow and the ceiling too short to get up and walk around comfortably, so everyone stayed seated for the hour-long flight.

After a time, Claire's curiosity got the better of her and she turned slightly to catch a glimpse of Jim in the back of the plane. He sat on the aisle, like her, so she could see he was dressed casually in khaki pants and a green polo shirt. His hair was cut perfectly, long enough to show off the waves, but short enough not to look shaggy. And he was already tan. Claire wondered how a man who worked indoors and lived in Minnesota could be tan in the winter. Obviously, he went to a tanning salon. It was probably Diane's idea. Claire couldn't get a view of Diane in the window seat beside Jim. Claire was certain Diane would be dressed brightly in a tight outfit and have a golden tan of her own. After all, she was only thirty years old. Jim had married her when she was a mere twenty-six and he was forty-one. It was obscene.

Jim raised his hand and waved at Claire, making her turn around hastily. Her face burned red. She hadn't realized she'd been staring at him for so long. Claire grabbed her charm bracelet and began twirling it around her wrist. She felt stupid for being so obsessed with her ex-husband. In truth, she shouldn't give a fig about him or that woman he married. But being around them still made her so nervous, she tended to act like an idiot.

Four years ago when Jim left her for Diane, it had taken Claire by utter surprise. She'd literally been the wife who was the last to know her husband was having an affair. She'd thought their marriage was fine. They'd been together for twenty years, raised a daughter, and both had interesting careers that they enjoyed. At the time, Claire's boutique was still getting off the ground, but making a small profit and growing. Sure, Claire had spent many hours there, sometimes all day and into the evenings to save on employee expenses when she was first starting out. Often, Mandy worked there, too, after school and on weekends. But Jim had been working a lot of overtime, too, so Claire hadn't felt bad about it. They were building their lives like couples do, or so she thought. She had no idea that Jim had decided to build his life elsewhere, with someone else.

For Claire, the day Jim told her he was leaving her seemed just like yesterday. It was still fresh in her mind and her heart. How could someone who vowed to love you forever suddenly want to leave? Maybe that was why she was still nervous around him and Diane. And now, she'd be spending the next seven days on an island with the two people who she least wanted to spend time with.

As the rest of the wedding party chatted around her, Claire closed her eyes and focused on staying calm. "I can do this, I can do this, I can do this," she chanted softly to herself.

"Mom."

Claire's eyes flew open. Mandy had turned in her seat and stared directly at her.

"What are you doing?" Mandy asked, frowning. "Are you okay?"

Claire stopped rocking in her seat and sat up straight. She hadn't even realized she'd been doing it. "I'm fine, dear. Sorry," she said, sheepishly.

Mandy pursed her lips. "Mom, you have to get ahold of yourself. You're scaring that poor gentleman beside you." With that, Mandy turned around in her seat again.

Claire grimaced. She looked over at her seatmate. "Sorry," she told him.

The elderly man smiled. "No worries," he said. "Are you afraid of flying?"

Claire shook her head. "No. Flying is fine. More like afraid of spending the next week with my ex-husband and his new wife." Claire tipped her head in the direction of the back of the plane and the elderly gentleman turned and looked at Jim through the separation between their seats.

"Oh, I get it. Do you want me to kiss you passionately and make him jealous?" he asked with a sly grin.

Her hands flew over her mouth as Claire stifled a laugh. "No, thank you," she said through her smile. "But it was a kind offer."

The man winked and turned back toward the window.

Claire took a deep breath and let it out slowly. The old man's silly offer had helped her relax. But, inside her head, she was still chanting, *I can do this, I can do this.*

* * *

From his seat at the back of the plane, Jim could watch everyone in the wedding party. He'd purposely boarded the plane early so he could get on without any questions from Mandy. Soon enough, he'd have to explain why Diane wasn't with him. He just wasn't sure yet what he was going to say.

To admit to his daughter that he'd failed at his second marriage after leaving her mother for Diane left a lump in his throat. What an idiot he'd been. The grass hadn't been greener on the other side. In fact, it had been brown, prickly, and downright nasty. When he'd left Claire to start a new life with Diane, he'd thought it would be a life full of love, laughter, and carefree fun. Boy, had he been wrong. The minute he'd said "I do," Diane ran over him like a steam shovel. She'd wanted a brand-new house, brand new furniture to fill it with, and expensive vacations. She'd wanted to change the way he dressed, the way he cut his hair, the way he ate, and even the way he walked. What the hell was wrong with the way he walked? Diane became a living nightmare. And the fact that they worked in the same office and that he was her superior didn't help matters. She thought she could reign over him at work like she did at home. But the worst part of all, she'd done everything she could to keep him away from his only child. That had hit Jim hard. When Mandy began planning the wedding, Diane flat-out refused to go on the island vacation and attend the wedding. They fought over it endlessly. He literally had to bribe her to agree to go to the engagement party by giving her a ridiculously expensive diamond necklace. It was all too much for Jim. When Diane refused to go to the wedding during their umpteenth argument six months ago, it was the final straw for Jim. He gave her an ultimatum. Go to the wedding with him, or leave. She chose to leave, thank God. As bad as it sounded, he'd actually been relieved.

Jim looked up in time to see Claire staring back at him. He gave her a small smile and a wave, which made her turn around instantly. Jim sighed. He'd really screwed up his life the day he'd left Claire. True, their marriage had been faltering and it had seemed like their work life had become more important than their relationship. Looking back, however, he realized that it had been his fault completely since he'd let himself become distracted with a younger woman at work while Claire had stayed true.

Jim watched the back of Claire's head as she seemed to be rocking in her seat and chanting something. Then he saw Mandy turn around in her seat and say something to her mother. Jim wondered what Claire had been doing. She seemed nervous. He'd secretly watched her as she'd boarded the plane with the rest of the group and was amazed at how young and vibrant she looked. She'd grown out her sandy blond hair a little and she looked like she'd lost a little weight. Not that Claire had ever been overweight; she'd always looked neat and trim. But today, she looked amazing in a pair of jeans and a T-shirt. Since the day they met in college, Claire had always been a smart, confident woman who knew what direction she was heading. Jim had always envied that about her. But today, she looked nervous, almost vulnerable. He wondered if she was, or if it was just his imagination.

As the plane landed in Marsh Harbour, James decided he'd keep his divorce to himself for as long as he was able. There was no sense dumping that information onto a fun family vacation and Mandy's special day. He'd make up an excuse for Diane's absence. He was pretty sure that no one was going to miss her anyway. He sure as hell knew he wasn't going to.

Chapter Four

There was a bustle of activity once the plane landed in the small Bahamian airport in Marsh Harbour. The group disembarked, picked up their carry-ons, then waited while the larger bags were unloaded. Soon they were going through customs where two pleasant local men asked them a few questions before sending them on their way. Throughout it all, Claire was near the front of the group and Jim was at the back, so there was no time for them to exchange words.

Taxis in the form of minivans waited outside to take people to their next destination. Their group needed to get to the ferry that would take them to the tiny island in the Abaco chain where they were staying. Claire, Mandy, Craig, Kaylie, Mark, Glen, and Lisa squeezed into one van while the others all piled into another. After a short drive, the friendly woman driver deposited them at the ferry office.

Claire took charge and bought tickets for the group to ride the ferry. Everyone left their luggage for the handlers to load onto the ferry and they all went outside into the beautiful Bahama sunshine to enjoy the warm weather. After coming from mucky snow and forty-degree days, the eighty degrees here was a welcome relief to them all. Everyone's spirits were rising at the idea of spending seven full days in paradise.

They all walked down to the dock and that was when Claire noticed Jim for the first time. He came bounding down to the dock and wrapped Mandy into a big bear hug.

"Dad! Finally," Mandy squealed. Father and daughter hugged, which made Claire's heart swell. True, she wasn't thrilled he was here, but she was happy he was here for Mandy.

As they hugged, Claire discretely looked around for Diane. Claire wondered where she was hiding.

"Hello, Claire," Jim said, coming up beside her. They hugged awkwardly, more for show than from affection. Claire felt how solid and in shape he was.

"Hi, Jim," was all Claire managed to say.

Jim went around the group saying hello, shaking hands with Craig and his parents, and giving out hugs to Lisa and Kaylie. Glen slapped him on the back as a good-natured greeting.

"So, old man, how are you doing?" Glen asked. Both men were of almost equal height and equal age and both had easy-going personalities. When they were married, Claire and Jim had always had a fun time visiting with Glen and Lisa.

"Old man, eh?" Jim replied, grinning at Glen. "You're just as old as I am, so watch it."

Claire frowned as she watched the two men interact. She suddenly realized just how much she missed family get-togethers like this, and it made her sad that they weren't the same anymore since the divorce.

"Just like old times, isn't it?" Lisa said to Claire as she came up beside her.

Claire smiled over at her sister-in-law. Lisa was the same height as Claire, but her hair was dark brown and cut at chin length for ease of style. Lisa lived the San Diego lifestyle to the fullest when she wasn't working as a paralegal in a law firm. She ran every day and played tennis and surfed. Her lean, muscular body showed how much work she put into it.

"Yep. Just like old times," Claire said, wrapping her arm around Lisa's waist in a hug.

A ferry worker announced that they'd be leaving in five minutes. The wedding group came together at the end of the dock to board.

"Daddy? Where's Diane?" Mandy called out to her father. Claire looked up in time to see an odd look cross Jim's face. He walked over closer to Mandy. Claire inched over toward them to hear what he was saying.

"I'm sorry, honey, but she decided not to come," Jim told her quietly.

Claire almost clapped her hands in delight, but then decided that wouldn't be appropriate and stayed still.

"Why not?" Mandy asked, apparently not willing to let the subject go.

Jim took a deep breath. "Well, sweetie, I just think she didn't feel comfortable spending an entire week with our family."

"That's ridiculous," Mandy shot back. "We've done everything possible to make her feel welcome. What more does she want?"

Jim stepped closer to Mandy. "Don't let it upset you, dear. It's not about you, believe me. Let's not let her ruin our good time here, okay?"

Mandy nodded then turned toward Craig and walked away. It was obvious she wasn't happy with this new development. Claire understood how she felt. After all, everyone, Claire included, had been kind to Diane despite the situation. How dare Diane act as if she were the persecuted one.

Jim just stood there, looking lost. For some unknown reason, Claire felt badly for him. She walked over and spoke quietly. "I'm sorry Diane isn't coming."

Jim turned to Claire and tossed her one of his rakish grins. "Are you? Really?" he asked. Then he winked, turned, and followed behind Mandy and the rest of the group.

Anger rose inside of Claire. Here she was, trying to be nice, and he had the nerve to question her sincerity. And with that damn grin of his. No man, especially one his age, had the right to look so damn cute when he was pissing her off. He was intolerable.

They all finally boarded the ferry, which was packed to the brim with people and luggage. All four rows of padded bench seats were full by the time everyone sat down. Jim had been one of the last men on because he played the gentlemen and helped the ladies in their group step up on the unsteady ferry. When he offered Claire his hand, she'd accepted, rolling her eyes. She didn't want his help, but she also didn't want to slip and fall into the water, either.

Their group sat together in a line, each couple sitting together. By the time Jim came to sit, the only spot left was next to Claire.

"Do you mind?" he asked, pointing to the small spot left on the end of the bench beside her. "Looks like it's the last seat on the ferry."

Claire sighed, but scooted over as close as she could next to Mandy. Everyone on the bench shifted to make room.

"Thanks," Jim said with a smile.

The ferry took off and was soon speeding out in the open ocean, heading to the island. Everyone in their group started to get excited about seeing the little island for the first time. When Mandy and Craig had chosen to be married in the Bahamas, neither one of them had ever actually visited there. They'd first thought of going to a large resort, but then abandoned that idea when they found this lovely little island with a charming resort and adorable village. The island was only five miles long and half a mile wide and there were stretches of white sand beaches all around it. The couple had loved the idea of enjoying a quiet island experience instead of a busy, all-inclusive vacation resort.

Claire had like it, too, the first time she'd seen photos of it online. It was the exact type of place that suited Mandy's low-key personality, and Claire understood why they'd chosen this out-of-the-way place.

Throughout the ride, Claire was extremely aware of how close Jim sat next to her. His leg kept brushing against hers and their hips touched every time the boat hit a wave. Try as she might, Claire couldn't move any closer to Mandy to get away from Jim. Finally, she crossed her right leg over her left to avoid his leg rubbing hers. Mandy had looked over at her with a puzzled frown, but didn't say anything.

The island finally appeared and soon they pulled through a channel into a natural harbor that was surrounded three-quarters of the way by land. On one side stood a candy cane striped lighthouse and on the other were buildings and docks set among the lush vegetation. The ferry stopped at several large docks to let passengers disembark before it finally arrived at the Harbour View Lodge's dock where Claire and her group were staying.

Once Claire stepped off the ferry onto the dock, she looked around in utter amazement. After having just come from Minnesota with the snow still on the ground and the grey, wet days, the contrast of this lovely jewel of an island was breathtaking. Lush, green plants grew in abundance with flowers of bright pink, yellow, and red blooming profusely. Palm trees, both short and tall, swayed in the gentle breeze, and all the buildings were painted cheery tropical colors of aqua, yellow, blue, pink, and green. Golf carts sped down the narrow streets, because cars were not allowed on the island. To call this place paradise was an understatement. It felt more like Heaven.

"Amazing, isn't it?" Jim asked as he came up beside her. Claire turned and nodded, smiling, until she realized who she was smiling at.

"Yes, it's beautiful," she said, letting her smile fade. She wasn't going to waste a good smile on him.

"Come on, Mom, Dad," Mandy called, waving them up the dock. "The lodge is this way."

"After you," Jim said, sweeping his arm in front of Claire. Claire walked ahead of him and caught up with the group right behind Janice and Carl. They crossed the street and walked under the painted archway that quaintly announced Harbour View Lodge, and then headed up the flight of cement stairs that led up the hill to the resort. Employees from the resort drove their luggage up and around the back and would carry it to their rooms.

The stairs led them to an open patio area that was surrounded by palm trees and flowering bushes and overlooked the lovely little harbor filled with yachts and sailboats anchored of shore. Towering above the patio was the three-story lodge where rooms had both a harbor and ocean view. The building was painted white with a dark blue trim. It all had a feel of an old-time resort from the 1940s. There was a breezeway that went between the lodge and restaurant, and from there a cheery, round woman dressed in bright, tropical colors came out and welcomed them.

"You must be our Minnesota wedding party," she said. "My, my, but look at all the blonds and blue eyes we have here."

Everyone in the group laughed.

Another woman came out wearing a yellow, floral dress that made her brown skin glow. She carried a tray of filled champagne glasses.

"This is Aneese," the first woman said, "And my name is Sandra. Welcome. I'm the resort's manager. Feel free to come to me with any questions or concerns you may have. Aneese manages the restaurant and the bar. Why don't you all just sit out here and enjoy the champagne and I'll just talk to the bride and groom and their parents for a minute to get the rooms set up."

The group of young people along with Glen and Lisa all accepted a glass and Claire followed Mandy and Craig along with Jim and the Fishers into the office where Sandra had led them. Sandra sat down at her desk, and opened her laptop computer.

"Now, let's see. We have two cottages reserved, one cabana, and three lodge rooms," Sandra said, looking at her computer. "The bride and groom have a cottage and so do Glen and Lisa Goodwin, is that correct?"

"Yes," Mandy said. Sandra gave Mandy the keys for both cottages and told her where they were located, down near the beach.

"Now, Mr. and Mrs. Fisher. I take it you're the groom's parents?"

"Yes," Janice answered.

"I see you have a lodge room. Here's your key, it's on the second floor. It's a lovely room, I'm sure you'll be very comfortable there."

Sandra started handing out more keys to Mandy and Craig to give to their friends. Cameron and Angela had a cabana down near the pool and Kaylie and her boyfriend had a room on the third floor.

"Now," Sandra said, smiling up at Claire and Jim. "That just leaves the bride's parents, Mr. and Mrs. Martin."

Claire frowned. *Why was this woman putting their names together?*

Sandra handed Jim a key. "Your room is also on the third floor. It's 3A. You're going to love this room. It has a balcony and a lovely view of the ocean, and of course all the rooms have a harbor view as well."

Claire stood silent a moment. *What about her key?*

"Well, that's it. Be sure to let me know if you need anything at all," Sandra said. "And tomorrow when you get a chance, pop in and we'll finalize the wedding plans for Saturday."

Claire looked over at Mandy. Mandy looked back at her, confused.

"Um, we need one more room," Mandy said. "My mom booked a third-floor room, too."

Sandra blinked. She looked from Jim to Claire. "I'm sorry. Aren't you the bride's mother?"

"Yes," Claire said. "But I have my own room. It was booked under my name, Claire Martin."

Sandra walked back to her desk and peered at her computer. "It says here there is a room for Mr. & Mrs. Jim Martin. It was originally a cottage, but then Mr. Martin called to cancel the cottage and requested the room instead."

Mandy stepped over to the desk. "Yes, that was for my Dad and his wife. But my Mom also booked a room for herself. It was with the original room bookings."

Sandra stared at her computer as if an answer would come to her. She bit her lip. "I'm confused. Isn't Mrs. Martin your mother?"

"Yes, she is," Mandy said. "But my parents are divorced. There is another Mrs. Martin who was supposed to share the room with my Dad, but she didn't come after all. My parents need separate rooms."

Claire watched and listened to the whole exchange growing more and more nervous. She grabbed her charm bracelet and began slowly twirling it on her wrist.

"I'm sorry," Sandra said. "I'm not sure how it happened, but when Mr. Martin switched from the cottage to a room, it must have been assumed he would be in Mrs. Martin's room.

We had no idea there were two Mrs. Martins."

Claire's eyes grew wider by the minute.

"Then we'll need another room," Mandy said calmly.

Sandra looked up at her with a strange look on her face. "You don't understand. We have no more available rooms. The lodge is booked solid for the entire week. We have three wedding parties here, and all the rooms, cabanas, and cottages are full."

Mandy looked over at her mom, a panicked look on her face. Claire stepped up to the desk. "Well, there must be something," she said. "I mean, you can't expect me and Jim to share a room. Are you sure you're booked full? Maybe there's just a mistake in the computer."

"I'm sorry, but there's nothing left," Sandra said again.

"What about another hotel or resort on the island?" Jim spoke up. "There must be an empty room somewhere nearby."

Sandra bit her lip again. "I'm afraid all three resorts on the island are booked solid. I just called everyone this morning for another party and there isn't an empty room on the island."

"Oh, you can't be serious," Claire exclaimed, starting to lose her composure. "There must be *something* on the island. How can there be no rooms?"

"I'm sorry, Mrs. Martin," Sandra said, looking distraught. "I'm sure there are house rentals available on the island, but they can cost between two to five thousand dollars a week."

"Fine," Claire said, looking over at Mandy. "Your dad can rent a house."

"Mom, are you kidding? That's too much money," Mandy said.

"What else is he going to do?" Claire asked, her voice rising.

Jim stepped up beside Claire and Mandy. Calmly, he said, "I'm not sure a rental house is the answer. What about another island close by?"

"Oh, maybe there's a hotel or resort back at Marsh Harbour that has an open room," Sandra said. "Would you like me to check?"

"No," Mandy exclaimed. "Dad. I want you on the same island as us, not a twenty-minute ferry ride away.

In the back corner of the office, Claire noticed that Janice and Carl were getting uncomfortable with the situation. Craig noticed it, too.

"Why don't I go help my parents settle into their room while you all hash this out?" he asked, but didn't wait for a response. The three Fishers left the room immediately.

Mandy took her mom's arm and pulled her aside. "Mom, I know this is crazy, but would you even consider sharing a room with Dad until something opens up?"

Claire's mouth dropped open. She couldn't believe her ears. "No. Are you kidding me? No. Absolutely not."

"But Mom," Mandy began.

"No, Mandy. Are you crazy? Share a room with your father? There has to be another alternative." Claire turned to Jim who just stood there, looking like he didn't know what to say. "Jim. You can't possibly want to share a room, either. What would Diane think? It's out of the question. Right?"

Jim looked from Mandy, who had a determined look on her face, to Claire, who looked panic-stricken. "Well, it wouldn't really be that bad, would it? Just for a few nights? I mean, they must have a cot I can sleep on, or something."

Claire couldn't believe what she was hearing.

"Oh, yes, we do have a cot we can put up in your room, Mrs. Martin," Sandra broke in. "And the room is large enough so it shouldn't be a problem."

"Oh, my God. No. No, no, no!" Claire looked out the office window at the resort grounds and the beach and ocean beyond. Her beautiful vacation in paradise was slowly turning into the vacation from hell.

"Mom, please," Mandy begged. "You two are the only ones who aren't a couple. It only makes sense that you share the room. Otherwise it will ruin everyone else's vacation."

Claire was listening, but just barely. Off in the distance, swaying gently between two palm trees, was an empty hammock. Claire turned to Sandra. "The weather here is always beautiful, isn't it? There's a lovely hammock out there. Jim can sleep outside and be just fine. Right?"

Sandra, Mandy, and Jim all looked at her as if she were crazy. At that very moment, Claire felt like she was going insane.

"Mom, you can't possibly expect Dad to live outside for seven days and nights," Mandy said sharply.

Silence filled the room. Claire felt like a trapped animal. She spun the charm bracelet on her wrist at warp speed. Jim stepped up beside Claire and placed his hand over her wrist to stop the jingling of the charms. Claire looked up into his vibrant blue eyes, searching for malicious humor. Instead, she saw sincere warmth radiating out from them.

In a calmer voice, Mandy said, "Mom, I know I'm asking a lot. Could you please share a room with Dad until another one becomes available? Please? For me?"

Claire looked over at Mandy, who looked like she was about to disintegrate into tears. She glanced at Jim again, who did in fact manage to look contrite about the whole incident. She really didn't have much choice, given how Mandy had asked.

"Fine," Claire said, feeling defeated. "Fine."

Sandra went into action, calling on the phone for a cot to be placed in 3A. "I really am very sorry about this entire incident," Sandra told Claire specifically. "Your room will be free for the entire stay. I don't know how this error occurred, and I am so sorry."

Claire just nodded. She didn't care how it happened, it just had. And now her vacation was going to be ruined.

"Thanks, Mom," Mandy said, giving her a hug. Claire let her hug her, but she wasn't very pleased with any of the people in the room right now.

The group turned and walked out the door with Mandy leading and Jim in the rear. He touched Claire's arm just as they stepped outside.

"I'm sorry this happened," he said softly. "Thanks for not letting me sleep outside."

Claire turned and glared at him, wondering if that was supposed to be funny, because she wasn't amused.

Chapter Five

Their luggage was in the room by the time they made it up the three flights of stairs. Claire watched Kaylie and Mark enter their room just down from their own. *Great. Their room is right next door to ours.*

Ours. Claire was angry just thinking that word. The room was supposed to be hers. Now it was theirs.

When Claire entered the room, she saw that the workers had already brought up the cot, and she glared at it. It was still folded up and just stood there, mocking her. She hoped it would fold up on Jim in the middle of the night.

Taking a deep breath, Claire looked around the room. It was a lovely room, despite her having to share it. The wooden plank walls were painted white with an aqua trim around the doors and windows. The furniture was made of brown wicker, as was the ceiling fan above the king-sized bed. Covered in a tropical scene bedspread, the bed sat in the center of the room, flanked by nightstands and lamps. In an alcove at the foot of the bed was a dresser and mirror, and on either side of that were small closets. On the far wall were glass patio doors that slid open and led out to a balcony. The balcony was big enough for two wooden Adirondack chairs. They were painted yellow and a table sat between them. Everything just shouted out tropical, and it was charming as could be, but the best part of the entire room was the view. Claire could see out past the pool area, past the outdoor bar and grill restaurant, and beyond to the white sand beach and the breathtaking aqua-blue ocean. It was so beautiful, it looked more like a painting than reality.

"It's beautiful, isn't it?" Jim asked, reiterating Claire's thoughts aloud.

Claire rolled her eyes. She'd forgotten in that one moment of happiness that Jim was in the room with her. She turned around, picked up her suitcase, dropped it on the bed, and opened it up. She was rewarded with a mess. Obviously, some TSA agent had a hay day digging through her suitcase.

Jim walked around to the other side of the bed and pushed his suitcase over by the cot. "I'm going down to the bar by the pool and ordering a Piña Colada. Want me to get one for you, too?"

Claire looked up at him through narrowed eyes. "No, thank you. You know I don't hold alcohol well. I'm going to change and go for a walk on the beach." She dug around in her suitcase and pulled out a tank top and a pair of tan shorts.

Jim leaned over and pulled a bikini top out of the messy bag. "Don't forget this," he said, winking.

Claire grabbed it away from him. "Leave my stuff alone," she ordered. She spun on her heel and walked into the small bathroom, slamming the door. She heard Jim chuckle as he left.

Looking into the framed mirror over the bathroom sink, Claire sighed. She looked a hundred years old after the long flight and the stress of sharing a room with her ex. She'd freshen up her makeup, pull her hair back, change, and then go down.

Even though the room had an air conditioner running to keep it cool, Claire felt a trickle of sweat run down her ribs from under her bra. She looked at the bikini top she'd grabbed away from Jim. Hmmm. A swimsuit top under her tank would be much more comfortable in this heat than a bra. She decided she'd wear it after all.

* * *

Jim went down the stairs at a fast clip, smiling the entire way. The face that Claire had made when she'd snatched her swimsuit top away from him was a cross between librarian prissy and murderous hatred. He couldn't help it. It made him chuckle. Claire had always been the one in their relationship to have a clear head and steady nerves. He'd never known her to be anything but calm, controlled, polite, and charming. But if today was any indication, she'd changed over the past four years—a lot. The way she'd nervously spun that charm bracelet around her wrist had almost scared him. He thought her hand would fall off. And the biting sarcasm that came out of her mouth was scary, too. She seemed so angry. Of course, he understood that their sharing a room was completely ridiculous, but there had been no other choice. The old Claire, at the very least, would have just made the best of it. This new Claire looked like she was capable of killing him in his sleep.

Some of the wedding party was already down by the pool drinking colorful, slushy drinks and enjoying the evening ocean breeze. Jim waved at them, then headed to the bar and ordered two Piña Coladas, one regular and one virgin.

Mandy came over to the bar while Jim waited for his order. "How is Mom doing?" she asked, biting her lip.

Jim smiled. "She's angry and resentful, but she'll survive. Your mom's a tough woman."

Mandy grimaced. "She was so looking forward to enjoying this vacation. I hope this won't ruin it for her."

Jim patted Mandy's arm. "Don't worry, dear. I will do everything I can not to ruin your mom's vacation. I know she'd feel bad if you worried too much and didn't enjoy it yourself."

When the two drinks came, Mandy frowned at her dad.

"Double fisting it, Dad?"

Jim laughed. "No. I ordered one for your mom. A peace offering of sorts. She should be down in a minute."

"She doesn't drink alcohol very often," Mandy said.

"I know. This one is virgin."

They joined the others at the table by the pool. Craig explained that his parents were still in their room, settling in. Kaylie and Mark were there drinking Margaritas, and Cameron and Angela were drinking beer. Glen and Lisa showed up and soon had frosty drinks in their hands as well.

A few minutes later when Claire walked over to the table, Jim couldn't help but watch her. She had on a simple outfit of shorts and a tank top, with the swimsuit top under it, he observed with a grin, and she'd pulled her blond hair back into a ponytail. Her legs looked long and toned, and the ribbed tank top accentuated her small waist. He couldn't help but stare, she looked really good.

Claire's brows rose, directed at him. He quickly stopped staring and picked up the drink he'd ordered for her. "Piña Colada? he asked. When he saw she was about to say no, he added, "It's virgin."

Claire stared at him a moment, then her face softened. She reached for the drink. "Thanks." Even though she said the word, to Jim it sounded like she wasn't all that appreciative.

"I'm going for a walk on the beach. Anyone else want to go?" Claire asked. Everyone in the group mumbled a desire to just sit and finish their drinks. Glen, however, stood up.

"I feel like walking. Honey, do you want to go?" he asked his wife.

Lisa shook her head. "You two go ahead. I'll just sit awhile."

Claire set down her drink in front of Jim. "Thanks," she said again, then walked away with her brother toward the beach.

As Jim watched her walk away, he wondered what it would take to get on Claire's good side. He had a week to find out.

* * *

Claire and Glen walked over to the wooden stairs that led down to the beach and jumped off the last step to land in the sugary sand. Evening was approaching, so the tide was coming in and taking up a good chunk of the beach. Claire didn't mind. It was a beautiful, warm day and when the water did hit her feet, it felt good.

"I heard you had a problem with your room," Glen said after they'd walked a little way down the beach.

"The room is great," Claire said. "It's the ex-husband sharing it with me that's the problem."

Glen chuckled. "Yeah, that would be a bit sticky. Lisa and I talked about it, and we'd be okay with having Jim stay at the cottage with us. It's a good size, so we have room for him."

Claire cocked her head and looked at her older brother. "That's nice of you both, but I'm not going to let you ruin your vacation by adding another body to your room. Mandy was right, he and I are the only ones here who aren't part of a couple. It only makes sense we share the room."

Glen shrugged. "Okay. But if you change your mind, the offer's still on the table."

They walked farther down the strip of beach. The waves coming in had packed down the sand, making it easy to walk on. It amazed Claire that the island resorts were full, yet they were the only two people on the entire strip of beach. She figured that people must flock to the other beaches on the island.

"So, tell me how life is in San Diego," Claire said. "Are you still enjoying teaching college science, Professor?"

"Yes, I am. Can't complain. How is Mandy enjoying teaching second grade?"

"She just loves it. It's her second year at the charter school, and she enjoys teaching in the smaller classes. She had interned in a public school and she didn't like it as much. The money isn't too good, but Craig earns a good income as a computer programmer, so she can afford to work there."

"What about you?" Glen asked. "How's the boutique doing?"

Claire smiled up at her brother. He was always looking out for her, even from two thousand miles away. "It's doing quite well. Better than I ever imagined. When I started it ten years ago, I never imagined it would be turning the profit it is now. I was able to hire two new part-time employees to help out this coming summer. It's wonderful."

"That's great," Glen said. "And what about Steven? Are you still seeing him?"

"Oh, yeah, we're still together," Claire said without much enthusiasm. She hadn't told anyone about the engagement yet and still didn't know if she was going to accept his offer of marriage or not.

"But?" Glen asked.

Claire stopped walking and stared up at him. "But what?"

"It just sounded like everything was fine, but..."

Claire shook her head. "No buts. Everything is fine with Steven."

"Hmmm. Okay. If you say so," Glen said, moving off again down the beach.

Claire stared after him, wondering what he'd meant. Did her voice reflect the hesitation she felt about her relationship with Steven? She shook it off and ran to catch up with him. She didn't want to talk about Steven this week with anyone, and she was bound and determined to keep it that way. When she made her decision about the proposal, it would be hers alone.

Glen looked over at Claire mischievously. "Did you really suggest that Jim sleep out in a hammock the entire time we're here, or was Mandy exaggerating?"

Claire laughed out loud. "Yep. I really did."

Glen chuckled. "Wicked."

Claire and Glen walked back to the resort and met up with the rest of the group and they all decided to go to dinner at a casual eating place that Sandra recommended. It was just a short walk downtown from the lodge, so they all took off on foot. Tomorrow, they had several golf carts lined up for the entire week that they could use to explore the island. Tonight, they'd have to hoof it.

Walking downtown was another fun experience for the group of tourists. There were businesses and houses all along the narrow street, each one painted bright colors with yards separated by colorful flowering bushes, palm trees and other lush vegetation. White picket fences or vine covered archways sat in front of several homes. Even though the lovely loyalist-style cottages were close together, they each had the feel of a private yard because of the greenery. It was like walking through a village from a hundred years ago with children playing happily in yards or riding bikes down the streets and adults all waving hello to everyone they passed. Claire loved how friendly everyone was, and how small town this little gem of an island felt.

The group entered the Lighthouse View Restaurant and stepped out onto the large, covered patio dining area that was open all around and jutted out onto the water in the harbor. True to its name, from any table in the place you could view the candy cane striped lighthouse across the way.

The hostess quickly set up a table large enough to accommodate their group of twelve and everyone sat down in pairs. Claire maneuvered herself next to Mandy and across from Glen and Lisa, but since everyone was sitting as couples, she once again found herself next to Jim. Claire sighed. It was inevitable. They were going to be linked throughout this entire vacation.

Menus were passed out and everyone started talking about the local food and what they wanted to try while they were there. Of course, fish and other seafood dominated the menu, but Claire didn't mind. She enjoyed seafood, and fresh seafood was going to be a delight.

"Do they ever smile?" Jim whispered in Claire's ear as he discretely pointed his menu toward Janice and Carl Fisher.

Claire looked in their direction. Both Fishers frowned at their menus. It was Claire's guess that they weren't adventurous eaters and were trying to find something familiar to eat. She had to admit, they both looked uptight. While everyone else had worn their beach clothes and flip flops to dinner, Janice and Carl had dressed up. They not only looked out of place at their table, but also in the entire restaurant. The other diners were wearing what they'd worn to the beach or on their boats for the day. Everyone except the Fishers.

Claire pursed her lips. She wasn't really a fan of Craig's parents, but she wasn't going to be unkind about them, either. They could do whatever made them feel comfortable. "Don't be mean," she whispered back to Jim. "They just don't seem very comfortable here. This wasn't their idea of the perfect wedding. They wanted to have a church wedding at home and a reception at the country club."

Jim nodded. "Country club? As in golfing or tennis?"

Claire turned to him. "Golfing. Why?"

Jim winked at her in reply, which infuriated her.

After everyone had ordered, Claire watched Jim put on his most winning smile and speak up toward Carl at the other end of the table. "So, Carl. You're a golfer, I hear."

Carl looked up, surprised at being called upon. "Um. Yes, I am. Do you golf, Jim?"

Jim nodded. "I've been known to hit a ball or two around a course."

Claire rolled her eyes. Jim was an excellent golfer, or at least he'd been one when they were married.

"Maybe we should see if there's a golf course here," Jim suggested. Claire realized he was trying to put Carl at ease, and she thought it was nice of him.

"Daddy," Mandy interrupted. "There are no golf courses on this island. I think there may be one over near Marsh Harbour, but I have no idea what it costs to golf there."

"We can ask Sandra at the lodge," Jim suggested. "I'm sure Craig and some of the other people here golf. Glen, you still golf, don't you?"

"Sometimes. Not as often as I'd like. But I could try to keep up," Glen said.

At the end of the table, Carl cleared his throat. "That sounds like a nice idea, but I don't have my clubs along. I never golf without my custom-made clubs."

Craig looked uncomfortable. Claire guessed that he knew Jim was trying to make his father feel comfortable with the group but that his father wasn't interested. "My dad has a wonderful set of custom-made clubs. He really doesn't enjoy playing without them. It was nice of you to suggest it, though, Jim."

Jim sat back in his chair, smiled, and nodded. Under his breath, he said loud enough for only Claire to hear, "Snob."

Claire had just sipped her iced tea when he said it and almost spit it out in a laugh. She grabbed her napkin and covered her mouth as she managed to swallow the liquid.

"Are you okay, Mom? Mandy asked, patting her on the back.

Claire slid her gaze to Jim, then turned back to Mandy. "Yes. I'm fine. It just went down the wrong way." When the attention was off her, Claire turned toward Jim and hissed, "Be nice!"

Their dinner was delicious. Claire had tried the fish of the day, which was red snapper that had been rolled in a crushed almond and bread crumb mixture and deep fried. It had tasted amazing. Jim had tried the fried conch, which he insisted Claire take a bite of, too. Everyone tasted a bite of each other's food since most of it was food no one had ever tried before. Everyone except Janice and Carl. They had stuck to plain chicken and rice.

It was late and the sky was inky black when the group walked back to the lodge. The town had quieted down and there were hardly any people on the streets. Up above, the sky glittered with stars. The couples began splitting off, saying goodnight, and going their own way, most likely toward the beach where they could hear the waves and look up at the stars. The Fishers headed up to their second-floor room, and soon Claire and Jim were left on the patio in front of the lodge, alone.

"Want to go sit by the ocean for a while?" Jim asked.

Claire considered it, but then shook her head. "It's been a long day. I'm tired. I think I'll go up to bed."

"Yeah, that sounds good."

They walked up the flight of stairs until they were on their third-floor landing. Both stood at the railing for a moment, looking across the dark harbor bay and up at the sky lit like diamonds.

"It's too bad Steven didn't come," Jim said, ruining the quiet moment for Claire.

"Yeah. And it's too bad Diane didn't come," she said, not really meaning it.

Jim looked at her with those teasing eyes, but didn't say a

word.

Once inside, Claire took over the tiny bathroom and changed for bed. The long flight, the walk on the beach, and the delicious food had finally caught up with her. She was beat tired. She couldn't wait to crawl into bed. She washed her face, brushed her teeth, and stepped out of the bathroom in a T-shirt and boxer shorts.

Jim had already opened the cot and made it up with the sheets, blanket, and pillow they had provided. There was a small refrigerator in the room with complimentary water bottles in it which was now at the head of his bed. Above him was the air conditioner. Claire looked at it a moment, figuring he'd probably freeze being that close to the air, and she grinned. Better him than her.

Without a word, Jim went into the bathroom. Claire heard the water running. She moved her suitcase over to the chair by the patio window and dug through it. She pulled hangers from one of the small closets and hung up a few items so they wouldn't wrinkle. Earlier, she'd hung up the dress she was going to wear to the wedding to make sure it smoothed out before Saturday. She'd noticed that Jim had done the same with his light-colored suit and a few of his cotton shorts and casual shirts. She was pleasantly surprised and wondered when he'd learned to take care of himself. If they'd still been married, it would have been her job to hang up his clothes.

With a sigh, Claire stood at the patio window and looked out, but all she saw was darkness. She cracked open the window and heard the waves gently hitting against the shore. It was a nice, lulling sound, and she wanted to listen to it until she fell asleep so she left the window open. Closing the curtains, she turned and pulled the bedspread down and slipped in under the sheet and blanket.

Claire looked around the room again. There was no phone,

no alarm clock, and no television. Nothing to distract from paradise. She liked that. She grabbed her purse from the floor beside the bed and pulled out her phone. There was service on the island, but she'd been warned before coming here that calls would cost a fortune. She set the phone on the nightstand to use as a clock, turned off the light on her side of the bed, and laid down with a content sigh.

"Wow, that speaks volumes," Jim said, coming out of the bathroom.

"What?" Claire asked.

"That sigh. Either you're very tired or that bed is very comfortable"

"Both," Claire said. She looked up at him. "Don't you have any pajamas to wear?"

Jim looked down at his white T-shirt and briefs. "You know I hate pajamas. I've always slept like this."

"Yeah, but we're not married anymore and I shouldn't have to look at you." Claire made a face at him, although she really shouldn't be complaining, because he looked pretty good for an old guy.

Jim grinned at her. "What about you? Got anything flannel to wear?"

"Oh, go to bed." Claire rolled over to face the window. Soon, she heard the light flick off and then the creaking of the cot as Jim laid down on it. It creaked, then creaked some more. When she thought he'd finally settled, it started creaking again.

"What the heck are you doing over there?" Claire asked, annoyed. "That creaking could wake the dead."

"I'm trying to get comfortable," Jim said. "This isn't exactly the softest bed on the planet."

The creaking continued, stopped, then started up again.

"Oh, for God's sake. Stop moving and go to sleep," Claire told him.

The creaking stopped. The room was quiet except for the hum of the air conditioner. After a few minutes, Jim said. "I hear the ocean. Did you leave the window open?"

Claire nodded in the dark room, even though Jim couldn't see her. "Yes. I wanted to fall asleep to the sound of the waves."

"It's nice," Jim said.

They both lay there a moment, listening to the ocean waves and the gentle evening breeze. Then Jim turned again on the bed and made another awful creaking noise.

Claire couldn't help it. She didn't know if it was the long day, the fact she was stuck with her ex-husband in a hotel room, or if insanity had finally hit her. She started giggling. The giggling turned into full-fledged laughter and her laughter turned into hysterical laughter. She was laughing so hard, tears were streaming down her face and her nose was running.

"What is so funny?" Jim asked, sounding amused. "You sound like you're losing it."

"I am," Claire said between howls of laughter. "I'm losing it entirely." She reached over to the nightstand and grabbed a handful of tissues from the box sitting there. Wiping her eyes and blowing her nose, she tried to calm herself down. But then Jim moved in the cot again and Claire burst out in crazy laughter again.

"You're losing it, lady," Jim told her. "You're finally cracking up."

"I'm finally on a beautiful island vacation and I'm sharing a room with my ex-husband who is sleeping on a bed that creaks every time he takes a breath. What isn't funny about that?" Claire asked.

"I'm glad you find it so funny," Jim said, but he couldn't help but laugh, too. It was, after all, a ridiculous situation and that horrible bed didn't help. "You'd better watch out. You know you always get the hiccups when you laugh this hard."

Claire finally settled down after a few more swipes at her eyes and blowing her nose. The comment about the hiccups had sobered her up a bit. She was surprised he remembered it. But then, after twenty years of marriage, she guessed it would take more than four years apart to forget the small details every couple knows about each other.

"Okay. I'm done," she said, laying down again. "Goodnight."

Jim laid down on the cot again, and it creaked once more. Claire gave a little giggle. "Goodnight," Jim said. Claire couldn't see him, but he was smiling into his pillow.

Chapter Six

Claire was up and in the shower early the next morning. She, Mandy, Janice, and Kaylie were going to meet up with Sandra after breakfast to discuss the wedding plans and she wanted to be showered and cleaned up early enough so the women wouldn't have to wait for her.

Jim had still been sound asleep when she'd awoken. She couldn't even imagine how he'd slept on that cot. It was too narrow and too short for him. But it did make her laugh. At least he was suffering from having to share a room with her.

Claire stepped out of the small shower stall and wrapped herself in a large, white towel, then wrapped her hair up in a towel as well. She stood in front the mirror, trying to decide what to do with her hair. It was humid here, bearable but bad for the hair. And it was windy by the ocean. She decided she'd be wearing her hair up a lot while they were on the island.

A buzzing sound came from the other side of the door and it made Claire pause. Was that her phone? She had told everyone she knew not to call her here because calls were crazy expensive. The buzzing continued. She was just about to go out into the bedroom to check it when she heard Jim's voice calling through the bathroom door.

"Lover boy is calling. Do you want me to answer it?"

In a panic, Claire ran out into the bedroom and snatched the phone away from Jim. "Don't you dare!" she screeched at him.

Jim chuckled.

Claire looked at the phone. It was Steven. Mustering up excitement, she answered. "Hi, Steven."

"Hello, Claire," Steven's calm voice came over the line. "I just wanted to make sure you arrived there safely."

Claire eyed Jim who was lying on her bed. *What the hell was he doing on her bed?* She turned toward the wall. "Yes, we did. It was a long day, but it was worth it. It really is paradise here. I wish you'd come, too."

"That's good to hear. How is your room?" Steven asked, seemingly avoiding her reference to him being there.

Claire turned a bit and glanced at Jim. *The room would be perfect if I weren't sharing it with my ex.* "It's fine," she told Steven. "There's a lovely view of the ocean."

"Wonderful." After a moment, Steven continued. "Have you thought about my proposal?"

Claire closed her eyes and took a deep breath. Of course she'd thought about it. A lot. But she still didn't have an answer. "Yes, I've been thinking about it," she said softly. "We can talk more when I get back."

"Okay. That's good," Steven said, sounding happy. "If you're still considering it, then you still might say yes. I know this call is expensive, so I'll let you go. I just wanted to make sure all was well with you."

Claire softened. It was so like Steven to care enough to check on her. She should be happy—no she should be honored to be with a courteous man like him. She turned and eyed Jim. Unlike someone else she knew.

"Thank you, Steven. You are always so thoughtful."

"Have a wonderful time and congratulate Mandy and Craig for me."

"I will. See you in a few days. Goodbye." Claire clicked off the phone.

Slowly, Claire turned around and stared at Jim. "What are

you doing in my bed?"

Jim sat up against the extra pillows on the side Claire hadn't slept in. "I'm not *in* your bed, I'm *on* it. See?" He grinned. "I figured you weren't in it, and that cot is murder on my back, so I thought you wouldn't mind if I just lay here."

Claire rolled her eyes. "You could have at least given me some privacy when I was talking to Steven. And, in no way are you to answer my phone. What in the world would Steven think if you answered my phone in my room?"

Jim cocked his head. Even after a night's sleep, his wavy hair fell perfectly into place and his blue eyes were bright and mischievous. *Damn that man looked good no matter where or what he did.* It pissed Claire off.

"You mean you're not going to tell lover boy that we're sharing a room?" Jim asked.

"Stop calling him that," Claire hissed. "And no, I'm not."

"Why not?"

Claire glared at him. "It's complicated."

"What's complicated?" Jim asked.

"Are you going to tell Diane?" Claire shot back.

The grin fell away from Jim's face. "Maybe. I don't know. She'll just have to deal with it," he said. A gleam returned to his eyes. "So, what are you thinking about?"

Claire frowned. "What?"

"You told lover...uh, I mean Steven that you were 'thinking about it'. What exactly are you thinking about?"

"It's none of your business," Claire told him.

"Ah, come on. If you don't tell me, I'll just have to call him and ask him myself."

"Don't you dare. You leave him alone."

Jim chuckled. "Come on. What is it you're supposed to think about?"

Claire sighed and sat down on the foot of the bed. "It's

complicated," she said again.

"You've already said that. What's complicated?"

She looked up at Jim. "Steven proposed to me the Saturday before I left."

Jim's expression turned serious. "Proposed?"

"Yes. Proposed. Believe it or not, there is actually a man on this planet who thinks I'm worth marrying," Claire said angrily.

Jim looked at her seriously. "I know you're worth marrying."

"Yeah, right," Claire said.

"So, where's the ring? Why aren't you excited about it?" Jim looked down at Claire's bare hand.

"It's back home. And I am excited about it. A little," she said honestly. "But I haven't said yes yet, so I didn't want to wear the ring."

Jim sat back against the pillows again and looked at Claire curiously. "You haven't said yes? Why not?"

"That's why it's complicated. I don't know if I want to get married again. Ever. You of all people should know why. It's not like my first marriage worked out so well."

Jim looked at Claire, a strange expression crossing his face. She couldn't tell if he was hurt, confused, or upset. "I don't think we had a bad marriage. We were happy for a long time," he said. "And we raised a beautiful daughter."

"So, you think we had a successful marriage even though it ended?" Claire asked.

Jim's eyes dulled. "You're right. It's complicated."

Claire nodded. "Yeah."

The air in the room hung between them, feeling heavy and suffocating. Neither one spoke. A minute ticked by. The air conditioner clicked on, snapping Jim and Claire out of their reverie.

"Don't say anything about the proposal to Mandy or anyone else," Claire told Jim. "This is Mandy and Craig's big week. Since I haven't said yes, there's no reason to mention it."

Jim nodded. "Okay." He smiled. "That's a nice outfit you're wearing. I like the whole head wrap thing you have going on there. Is that what you're going to wear to breakfast?"

Claire frowned, then looked down at herself. She was still wearing just a towel wrapped around her body. "Damn it. Why did you let me sit here in a towel? You are evil, you know that?" She jumped up, holding onto her towel and ran back into the bathroom with the sound of Jim's chuckle in her ears.

* * *

Jim lay on a towel on the beach, shading his eyes against the sun. He watched as Claire, Mandy, and Kaylie walked far out into the blue-green water on the sand bar. Good God, his back ached. That damned cot was worthless to sleep on, and now he was paying the price. He wasn't sure how he was going to survive sleeping on that torturous thing for six more nights.

Jim tried concentrating more on the warm sun and beautiful beach and less on his backache. Looking around, he was amazed at how few people populated this long strip of paradise. If this were a beach in California or Florida, it would be wall-to-wall people. But here, on this small island, there were only about fifteen people spread out along the beach and most of them were from their group.

During breakfast, down by the pool, everyone had decided to take the golf carts and drive the five miles down the island to Land's End beach. The waitress had told them it was the prettiest beach on the island, and at low tide they could walk far out into the water on the sand bars. So, after breakfast, and after the ladies had their meeting with Sandra about the wedding plans, everyone except Janice and Carl had hopped into golf carts and driven to Land's End. The Fishers had declined, saying they were going to explore the gift shops in the small town. Jim, however, figured their not coming along had more to do with Janice not wanting to dirty herself with sand and salt water. Even though Jim really liked Craig, he had a hard time liking Janice and Carl. Janice was too prissy and uptight for his liking and Carl was too full of himself. He was happy that they hadn't come along and ruined the fun.

Jim's eyes turned back to Claire standing beside Mandy and Kaylie in the water. The three women had picked up something from the water and were standing close together, examining it. The younger girls were wearing bikinis. Claire had on a bikini too, but she'd pulled on a pair of jean shorts over the bottoms. Jim wondered why. Even at the age of forty-five, Claire's body could hold its own against the younger girls. Jim smiled as he admired her long legs and narrow waist. If he didn't know any better, he'd think all three women were the same age.

Steven had proposed to Claire. That unwanted thought popped into his head out of nowhere. What in the world did Claire see in that stiff, egotistical, workaholic? Sure, Steven always said all the right things at the right time, but didn't Claire realize it was a show put on by a practiced salesman? Steven was a phony, through and through. Claire couldn't possibly want to marry a jerk like that.

But why do I care? I'm the one who left her. Those words came uninvited into Jim's head.

Jim lifted his body and propped himself up on his elbows, his lower back suffering the consequences of his actions. His eyes scanned the beach. Craig and his friend Cameron were out in the water, snorkeling. Mark was a short distance away from Jim, lying in the sun while Angela walked down the strip of beach looking for seashells. Glen and Lisa had gone on a beer run. But despite everything else Jim could have focused his eyes on, they still returned to Claire.

Jim thought back five years to when he started looking at Diane instead of Claire. He'd just turned forty-one, he was working all the time, and his daughter was grown and in college. Claire was always busy with her boutique, or so it seemed, and Jim found himself spending more time at the office and less time at home. He and Claire had been together for twenty years. They'd grown comfortable with each other. Too comfortable. They no longer etched out time to spend together as they had earlier in their marriage. There were no date nights, no dinners out, and no going to the movies. They saw each other in the morning before work and on Sundays when both were home and Mandy came home for dinner. As far as either of them knew, their marriage was typical of other couples their age. But then, Jim met Diane, and something changed.

Jim had felt he was growing old, and if he admitted it to himself, he'd been afraid of it. Diane, on the other hand, was only twenty-five, had a zest for life, and for some unknown reason had a crush on him. Instead of ignoring her, he'd enjoyed the attention of this younger, attractive woman who built up his ego and made him feel young again. She told him he was handsome, she laughed at his stupid jokes, and she was available. He fell hard for her, and had left Claire behind.

"Why?" he asked aloud as he sat alone on the beach.

"Why what?" Glen walked over with a cooler full of beer and plopped down beside Jim, offering him a bottle. Lisa waved at them and headed out to where Claire and the girls stood in the water.

"Nothing," Jim said in answer to Glen's question. "I was just talking to myself."

"Hmmm. Could be the first sign of heatstroke. Maybe we

should get you in the shade," Glen said with a grin.

Jim took a sip of beer and let his gaze trail off toward Claire again. She was laughing at something Lisa had said to her. He wished he could make her laugh again. With him, not at him like she had last night about the creaking cot."

Jim pulled himself up into a sitting position and made an old man grunt from the pain it caused his back.

"What was that coming from you?" Glen asked.

"That's the noise of an old man who slept on a cot last night," Jim told him. "And it isn't pretty."

Glen laughed. "That's what you get for divorcing my sister. It's karma, man."

Jim looked over at Glen. They hadn't spent much time together since the divorce, but when they were together for family events like Mandy's college graduation, Glen had always been nice to Jim. "Why don't you hate me for leaving Claire? You're her big brother. You should have punched me out."

"Well, I did think of it, but I figured your punishment was losing Claire. And if you were happier not married to her, then I guess I thought she'd be happier without you."

Jim stared at Glen. "Is she? Happier without me, I mean?"

Glen shrugged. "She has Steven now. You have Diane. People move on."

Jim turned to look in Claire's direction again. The women were walking back toward shore.

"You have moved on, right?" Glen asked.

Jim looked at Glen. "Huh?"

Glen pointed toward the women. "I have a feeling you're not watching Mandy, Kaylie, or Lisa. If it's Claire you have your sights on, watch out. You're married to Diane now. Claire is off limits."

Jim sighed. "Even if I had my sights on Claire, she'd be the first one to tell me off. So you don't have to worry."

"Good," Glen said. "Don't hurt her again, Jim. She deserves better."

Jim nodded. Glen was right. So why did it bother him so much?

* * *

Mandy and Claire walked slowly through the water on the sand bar toward the beach. Kaylie had gone ahead of them to lie on the towel beside Mark and Lisa had gone back to sit with Glen.

"How'd it go, sharing a room with Dad last night?" Mandy asked, concern in her voice.

"It was fine," Claire answered, trying to sound upbeat. She laughed. "The cot was the perfect revenge. He could barely walk this morning."

Mandy pursed her lips and stared at her mother. "Mom, that's terrible. I want Dad to enjoy this trip, too."

Claire sobered. "Sorry, hon, but you can't expect me to be happy about sharing a room with your dad. I'm trying to make it work, though."

Claire watched as a worried frown crossed Mandy's face. No one at only twenty-four years old should look that serious on her wedding week. "Don't worry, Mandy. We'll be fine. I was only teasing."

Mandy sighed. "It's not that. Craig and I got into a fight last night about me making you share a room with Dad. I guess his parents were upset about what happened in the office yesterday, and complained to Craig about it. Then he got all uptight about it, too."

Claire looked confused. "What were they upset about? They didn't have to share a room with your father."

"His parents don't like confrontation. It makes them nervous," Mandy said.

"No one likes confrontation, but you can't agree all the time," Claire said.

"I know. I think Craig's upset about how uptight his parents are acting and he's putting it on me. So, do you think you and Dad could just try to get along so no one feels uncomfortable?"

Claire sighed. "We're doing the best we can, sweetie. You and Craig shouldn't be worrying about us. Just have fun and ignore us if we get weird, okay?"

Mandy grinned mischievously. She looked so much like her dad when she grinned like that. "Honestly, I'd like to tell Janice and Carl to pull the sticks out of their asses, but I guess that wouldn't be very nice."

"You sound exactly like your dad," Claire said, laughing.

Mandy walked off to go sit beside Kaylie and Claire headed on down the beach where she'd left her things with Jim. She waved at Glen and Lisa who were lying on their towels a short distance away. The sun was high in the sky and her shoulders and arms felt hot already despite the heavy layer of sun block she'd rubbed on earlier.

Jim lay on his towel, his sunglasses covering his eyes, and a beer dug half-way into the sand beside him. He was already tanning, not burning like Claire. She always hated the way he could tan in a day, yet it took her all summer. And she had to admit, he looked good with his shirt off. She didn't remember him having such a muscular body when they were married. He must be working out.

Claire dropped a small, wet starfish she'd found on the sand bar onto his bare chest, then walked around to the other side where her towel was laid out.

"What the heck is that?" Jim howled when the coolness of the starfish hit him. He sat up suddenly and snatched it off his chest.

"It's just a starfish, silly," Claire said, giggling.

"Yuck. You know I don't like slimy things. Is it alive?"

Claire laughed. "You're such a baby. Of course, it's not alive, or else I wouldn't have taken it out of the water."

"Hmmm. It is cute," Jim said, inspecting it. "Here. Take it back." He gingerly handed it back to Claire. She set it carefully in the sand beside their towels.

Jim lowered his sunglasses. "Your shoulders and back are burnt. Here," he pulled himself up onto his knees with a small grunt of pain and picked up the bottle of sunscreen. "Come over here and let me rub more lotion on you."

Claire narrowed her eyes at him. She didn't really want him touching her. "That's okay. I'll just put on my shirt."

"You still need some lotion on so it doesn't peel. Come on. I promise I won't bite."

Claire bit her lip, but she kneeled on the towel in front of Jim and let him gently rub in the lotion. She had to admit, the lotion felt good on her tender skin.

"See now? It's not so bad," Jim said. Claire could almost feel him grinning at her. "You should be more careful here. You know you burn easily."

Claire started twirling her charm bracelet around her wrist. Having Jim touch her, especially so gently, made her nervous.

"There. All done." He reached around her and placed his hand over hers to stop her from jangling her bracelet. Then he lifted her arm up higher to inspect it. "I'm surprised you still wear this," he said softly.

Claire sat very still. Jim leaned over her from behind, and his breath tickled the back of her neck when he spoke. It unnerved her.

"Of course I still have it," she said, pulling her arm away from his grasp and moving over to her towel. She quickly slipped on the T-shirt she'd brought along. "You may have paid for it, but Mandy was the one who actually picked it out. And she's added to it through the years, see?" Claire pointed out the new charms. "Here's a pink dress to symbolize the success of the boutique, and here's a diploma to celebrate her college graduation."

Jim watched Claire intently as she pointed out the new charms.

"I'm glad you still wear it," he said. "For Mandy, of course."

Mandy and Craig walked over with their towels and gear packed up and slung over their shoulders. "Everyone's getting toasted out here, so we thought we'd better get out of the sun for the day. We're all going to hit a few of the outdoor bars on the way back to the lodge. You guys game?"

"Why don't you go with them, Jim? I can drive back to the lodge. I'm really not up to bar hopping right now," Claire said.

Jim looked up at his daughter. "You guys go ahead. We'll catch up with you." Mandy waved and off they went down the beach.

Claire looked confused. "Aren't you going with them?"

"No," Jim said, getting up and shaking out his towel. "We're both going with them. It'll be fun. You don't want to miss out on the fun, do you?"

"I'd rather just go back to the lodge and clean up before dinner. I'll drop you off where the kids are and you can catch a ride with one of them."

Jim waggled his brows. "Aw, come on, Claire. You don't have to drink to have fun. If you don't watch out, I'm going to have to call you Janice."

Claire narrowed her eyes at him.

"I promise," Jim said. "After the first stop, if you still want to go back to the lodge, we'll go. Deal?"

"Fine," Claire said, sighing. She felt like all she'd done this whole trip was give in.

Chapter Seven

Claire, Jim, Glen, and Lisa all sat at one end of the table at the Water's Edge Bar while the younger people sat around the rest of the table. They'd stopped at the Last Stop Bar & Grill first, then moved on to the bar at the Red Snapper Inn. This was the third place they'd stopped and the last before they would head back to the resort. Everyone was in good spirits, and even though Claire was the only one drinking virgin drinks, she was having just as much fun as the rest.

Claire watched Jim as he joked around with Craig's friend, Cameron. Cameron was a computer programmer like Craig, and he and Jim had literally nothing in common, yet Jim could always find common ground to talk about with anyone. Claire had always marveled at Jim's ability to do that. She swore that he could have sat at dinner with the President of the United States and have had an interesting conversation.

"Having fun?" Glen asked, leaning over toward Claire.

Claire smiled at her brother. He'd had a lot to drink, but it didn't show. He was a guy who could hold his liquor. "Yeah, I am. I didn't even want to come along, but now I'm glad Jim talked me into it."

"Hmmm," Glen said, turning his sights on Jim.

"What?" Claire asked.

"Oh, nothing. Have you heard from Steven since you got here?"

"He called this morning. I'd told him not to bother since it was so expensive, but he did anyway."

"He probably misses you," Glen said.

Claire looked out past Glen at the ocean view. Every place they'd gone today had an outside patio with an amazing view. "Probably," she agreed. "He's always thoughtful like that."

"That's good to hear. We should all get together sometime. I've only met him once."

Claire nodded, her eyes turning back toward Jim. She was surprised to see him look over at her, too, and he raised his glass to her in a silent toast. Claire smiled.

"Be careful, baby sister," Glen said, then got up to get another drink from the bar.

Claire stared after him. *What in the world did he mean by that?*

As the sun began to set, the group decided it was time to go back to the lodge. Craig started worrying about his parents, and that made Mandy anxious as well. Claire just wished the Fishers would relax so their son could.

They all walked over to the golf carts. Claire and Jim had been sharing one, so when they got to it, she put out her hand. "Hand over the keys. I'll drive back."

Jim didn't put up a fight. Claire figured he realized he'd had a bit too much to drink and his back still hurt, too.

It was only a five-minute drive to the resort and soon they were in their room again. Mandy had said they should all meet down at the patio in a half-hour to go to dinner. Claire hurried into the bathroom with clean clothes and quickly showered and changed. She wasn't sure where they were going to dinner, so she decided on white cotton pants and a silky blue camisole top. When she came out of the bathroom, she saw Jim had claimed one side of the bed again and was talking on his phone.

"It was nothing," he insisted into the phone. "I didn't even know she'd taken a picture." He paused, and Claire heard a screeching voice come through the speaker.

"What the hell do you care anyway?" Jim said. "Oh, just get over yourself."

Claire grimaced. She didn't want to hear this conversation. She grabbed her sandals and stepped out onto the balcony, closing the glass door behind her.

Claire stood on the balcony and looked out over the resort grounds. It was dark, but the grounds and walkways were lit up, as was the pool. People were down by the bar, and others sat on the porches of their cottages. She took in a deep breath, enjoying the aroma of tropical flowers and salty air. She was so absorbed in her surroundings that when the patio door slid open, it startled her.

"I'm off the phone now," Jim said gruffly. "You can come back in."

Claire turned and looked at him. "Trouble with the wife?" she asked, teasing.

Jim narrowed his eyes. "Just a misunderstanding," he said sharply. "Apparently Mandy took pictures this afternoon at the beach and posted them on her Facebook page. There was one of us from behind, when I was rubbing lotion on your back. We weren't even the focus of the picture, but Diane had a hissy fit about it."

Claire bit her lip. Divine justice, she wanted to say. The other woman now jealous of the ex-wife. But she saw how upset Jim was, so instead she just said, "Sorry."

Jim grabbed clean clothes out of his suitcase and looked up at Claire with piercing eyes. "Yeah. Sure you are," he said. He turned and headed into the bathroom, slamming the door.

Claire's face heated with anger. "Jackass," she said under her breath. Every time she tried being nice to him about Diane, he threw it back in her face. Fine. She wasn't going to be nice anymore. She went to the closet and grabbed the light jacket she'd brought along and then headed out the door and down to the patio.

Some of the group was already down there, waiting, so Claire sat down with Cameron's wife, Angela, and started up a conversation. Angela was a pretty girl with golden red hair, very pale skin, and light blue eyes. She was a registered nurse and worked in the pediatric department of a hospital in Minneapolis. Claire had noticed today at the beach that Angela had laid in the shade to protect her skin. She was a smart girl. Claire asked her about working with children and they fell into an interesting conversation about her nursing job.

Mandy appeared with Craig a few minutes later and they had a small huddle with their friends. Just as Jim came down the stairs, the rest of the wedding party left together, leaving only Claire, Jim, Mandy, and Craig.

"What's going on?" Claire asked Mandy.

Mandy glanced nervously behind her before answering. "I sent everyone else off to have dinner. We're waiting for Craig's parents."

Craig cleared his throat. "We thought it might be nice to have dinner with just the parents tonight," he said. Craig lowered his voice. "I think my parents are a little uncomfortable with being thrown into the whole crowd since they don't know anyone here but us. I thought if we had dinner in a smaller group, they might get to know you two better and be more relaxed."

Claire thought the Fishers were just unsociable and that's why they didn't feel like they fit in, but she kept that to herself. "That sounds nice," she told Craig with a smile. He seemed to relax a little when she agreed with him.

Jim didn't say anything. He still appeared to be in a foul mood from his conversation with Diane.

"Are you okay with that, Daddy?" Mandy asked.

Jim shrugged. "Doesn't matter to me," he said brusquely.

Janice and Carl came out of their second-floor room and

down the stairs. Mandy and Craig turned to greet them. Claire took this chance to kick Jim in the ankle. "Be nice tonight. The kids are under enough strain with Craig's parents."

Jim glared at her but didn't say anything.

"We thought we'd try the Blue Bay Grill downtown," Mandy said as they all stood there in a circle, staring at each other.

"Sounds good," Claire said. "What about Glen and Lisa?"

"Lisa said she was tired after today. They're going to grab a bite down at the pool bar and head back to their cottage," Mandy said.

Claire nodded. *Chickens.* "Well, shall we go?"

The group walked in twos down the narrow street. Mandy and Craig were in the lead, Janice and Carl were in the middle, and Claire and Jim brought up the rear. The two front couples had their arms linked, but Claire stayed as far away as possible from Jim. If he was going to be a jerk, then she was going to ignore him.

The Blue Bay Grill was busy, but their group found a table by the water and sat down. Just like the restaurant the night before, this one was a large, covered deck that jutted out over the harbor bay. Out in the harbor, they saw lights on several of the small boats and yachts. It was a relaxing setting to have dinner.

"I'll have a scotch and water," Jim said to the waitress when she came up to the table.

Oh, boy, Claire thought. He was no longer ordering the fruity island drinks. Tonight he was going to drink the hard stuff.

"Do you want a scotch, too?" Jim asked Carl loudly across the table.

Mandy's eyes darted between her father and mother. Claire shrugged. What could she do?

"I'll just have a beer," Carl said.

Janice ordered a glass of white wine, and Mandy followed suit. Craig ordered a beer like his father had.

"I'll just have iced tea," Claire told the waitress.

While they waited for their drinks, they perused the menu. Tonight there wasn't the easy banter they'd all enjoyed with the younger people the night before. No one was sharing ideas about the menu or what they wanted to try. To Claire, the atmosphere around the table seemed oppressive.

"What are you thinking of ordering, Mandy?" Claire finally asked, trying to get the group talking.

Mandy looked at her, relief filling her eyes. "The grilled tilapia with mango sounds good," she said. "And these Au Gratin potatoes it comes with sound delicious."

"They do. I might try that, too," Claire said. "What about you, Janice? Do you see anything you like?"

Janice looked up at Claire with a dry expression. "No. I don't see anything, yet."

"Well, maybe you need to look harder," Jim said.

Mandy's mouth dropped open and Janice looked at him with pursed lips. Claire glared at Jim, elbowed him in the side, and mouthed, "Stop it!"

The drinks arrived and Jim told the waitress to keep them coming. He picked up his drink and downed it in one long swig. Mandy stared at him in disbelief. Claire held her breath. Jim had never been a heavy drinker. Whatever Diane had said to him on the phone had really set him off. But she wasn't going to let him ruin their night and upset Mandy and Craig if she could help it.

After they ordered, Claire tried again to start a conversation. "Did you have an enjoyable day today?" she asked Janice.

Janice looked up at Claire in that controlled way she

regarded at everyone. She patted her short, processed, blond hair, even though every hair was in place and couldn't move from all the hairspray gluing it down. "Our day was okay," she said. "We walked around to the few gift shops they have here. I didn't really find much to buy, though."

Claire just nodded, not quite sure how to respond. *What did Janice expect to find? A shopping mall?* "Well, it was a lovely day out. Anything is better than the cold weather we came from."

Janice sniffed. "I thought it was a bit hot."

Out of the corner of her eye, Claire saw Jim start to open his mouth and she quickly kicked him under the table. He glared at her, but shut his mouth.

The waitress brought Jim another scotch and water and also two baskets of corn muffins for the diners.

"Oh, those smell heavenly. I'm starving," Claire said, reaching for a muffin.

Jim downed his drink and signaled for the waitress again.

Everyone except Jim tried one of the warm muffins. Claire thought they tasted delicious, but she noticed that Janice wrinkled her nose after a small bite and set hers down. *Good. More for me.*

"Is that coconut I taste in these?" Claire asked Mandy.

Mandy nodded. "Who would have thought coconut would taste so good in corn muffins?"

Craig agreed and took another one.

Janice pushed her plate away.

Another drink came for Jim, but this time Claire was quicker than he was. She grabbed it and set it out of his reach. "Why don't we just save this for after dinner?" she asked, staring hard at him.

Jim glared back at Claire.

Mandy spoke up. "Yeah, Daddy. You don't want to get sick, do you? Tomorrow will be another beautiful day."

Jim's face softened a little. "You're right," he said sweetly. Too sweetly. "Isn't it just wonderful, Carl, how the women in our lives have a way of telling us what to do?" He turned to Craig. "You just wait, my boy. You'll never have to think for yourself again."

Mandy's face paled.

"Jim!" Claire said angrily.

Craig just stared at Jim with a blank look on his face.

Carl spoke up. "Well, that may be true for you, Jim, but my wife never tells me what to do. Our marriage is an equal partnership."

Jim glanced at Carl, an amused look on his face. "Whatever you say, old boy."

Claire was so angry she could have pushed Jim into the harbor and held him under the water. She picked up the glass of scotch and slammed it down in front of him, sloshing liquid all over the tablecloth. "Here. Drink yourself to death for all I care."

Jim stared at her for one long moment, but didn't pick up the glass.

Claire was relieved when the food came and they could all pretend to be too busy eating to talk. Claire's meal was delicious, and Mandy said hers was, too. Craig didn't say anything about his and Claire guessed it was because he was too upset to enjoy it. She didn't know how to make things easier for Craig. She didn't understand why Jim was taking his anger out on everyone at the table, and Craig's parents were just plain difficult. She didn't envy Mandy for marrying into a family like that.

Although tonight their family wasn't any better.

Jim ate in silence, then ordered coffee when the waitress came around again. Claire noticed he hadn't touched the last drink, thank goodness. Maybe he was finally coming to his senses.

"So. What's on the agenda for tomorrow?" Claire asked as everyone finished up their meal.

Mandy spoke up. "Craig and I have to go over to Marsh Harbour on the early ferry to register for our marriage license. We should be back by early afternoon, though."

"Maybe we could all do something when we get back," Craig offered, but without enthusiasm. Claire figured that after tonight, he wanted to keep his parents as far away from her and Jim as possible.

"What are you and Carl doing tomorrow?" Claire asked Janice.

"We haven't made any plans yet," she said, tossing a sour look Jim's way.

Claire gave up on conversation. She was getting nowhere.

As soon as the Fishers were finished eating, they excused themselves from the table. "It's been a long day," Carl said. "Janice is feeling a bit chilled in this open air, too."

The air felt nice to Claire after the warm day. She figured Janice was one of those women who felt cold all the time. "Please stay," Claire said. "You can wear my jacket if you're cold," she offered to Janice.

The two Fishers stood. Janice wrinkled her nose. "No, thank you, Claire. We really should be off. I'm sure we'll run into you tomorrow."

Mandy looked at her mother, and then Janice, an uncertain expression crossing her face. Stay with her parents or leave with the Fishers? Claire's heart went out to her.

Craig made the decision for her. "Let's walk back with my parents," he said to Mandy. Mandy didn't look like she wanted to, but she nodded and stood up.

"Are you coming?" Mandy asked her mother, completely ignoring her father.

"I think I'll just sit here a while longer," Claire said. They all said goodnight and then they were gone.

Claire turned narrowed eyes on Jim. "What the hell were you thinking, acting that way? Why would you want to purposely upset Mandy and Craig?"

Jim didn't reply. He looked at his bill, put some money on the table, then stood. "Let's go," he said. Then he turned and walked away.

Claire had half a mind to throw a glass at him, but she refrained. She left money for her own meal and a tip, then followed behind Jim out into the dark, quiet street.

Jim walked briskly ahead of Claire and she had to run to catch up. At this point, she was so angry at him, she thought of locking him out of their room. The thought of being in that small room with him all night made her want to scream.

After a time, they came to a dock that jutted out into the harbor and was lit with tiny twinkle lights. Jim stopped, turned, and walked down the dock. Claire followed, although she had no idea why. At the end of the dock were benches on each side of it. Jim dropped down on one. Claire sat down on the other.

"Why are you so nice to those snotty Fishers?" Jim asked. "It's obvious they think they're better than we are. They annoy the hell out of me."

Claire frowned. "I'm nice to them, because I don't want to upset Mandy or Craig. We only have to be around the Fishers this one week and then we'll hardly ever see them. The real question is why were you such a jerk tonight?"

Jim sighed and ran his hand through his hair and down to the back of his neck. "Don't you ever get tired of people telling you what to do?"

The question took Claire by surprise. "What do you mean?"

"I have Diane harping at me from one side and my boss pushing me around on the other. I come here and I'm supposed to be nice to a couple of snobs who aren't nice to me. It's all so stupid, don't you think?"

Claire sat back against the bench. This wasn't the conversation she'd expected. She absently twirled her charm bracelet in circles around her wrist. "We all have to do things we don't want to sometimes. Sure, the Fishers are a pain, but our daughter is marrying into their family. We have to be civilized about it. And tonight, you were definitely not civilized."

Jim looked up at Claire. His eyes fell to her wrist. He reached over and placed his hand on the bracelet to stop it from spinning. "What is it with you and that bracelet? When did you become so nervous? And when did you start kowtowing to idiots? You were always so calm and confident when we were married. Now you have that annoying habit of spinning that noisy bracelet. What are you so damned nervous about?"

Claire's narrowed her eyes and drew her lips into a thin line. "Well, excuse me for not being perfect," she said. "How dare you judge me? Did it ever occur to you that maybe I changed after my husband of twenty years walked out on me without even the slightest bit of warning? You just came home one day and said, 'Oh, guess what? I found someone else I love better than you'. And then you sauntered out of my life, leaving me to figure out how I was going to manage."

"That was four years ago, Claire. You're doing fine. What are you so worried about?"

"Yes, I'm doing fine. I'm doing better than fine. But guess what? I didn't know I would be fine when you left. I suddenly had no security. I had to hope and pray that the boutique would make enough money so I could earn a living and keep the house. There was no longer a second income and no longer someone to lean on when life got hard. You took that all away when you went flitting off with your younger woman. But even with all that, the worst part was that I had no idea you were unhappy in our marriage. You never said a word. And you didn't love me enough to try to do anything to save our marriage. You just left. So, if you're wondering why I'm not the calm, confident woman I was years ago, then maybe you should think about whose fault it is. Because it definitely isn't mine." Claire stood and stormed up the dock and down the dark street toward the lodge.

* * *

Jim sat on the bench on the dock and watched as Claire ran down the street. He should go after her. He should make sure she made it safely back to the lodge. But he couldn't move. And he was pretty sure she didn't want him to follow her anyway.

Jim sat there listening to the sound of the water lapping softly against the dock. Claire was right. He'd been a real jerk tonight. No, he'd been an ass. A complete ass. He knew it the entire time he was acting that way in the restaurant, but he just couldn't seem to stop himself. He'd embarrassed Mandy, he'd embarrassed Claire, and he'd managed to make Craig and his parents angry at him. Shit. He'd managed to make everyone angry at him all in a matter of a couple of hours.

Jim thought back through the day. It had started out fine, despite waking up with a sore back. He and Claire were getting along. She'd let him rub lotion on her back this afternoon. And she'd actually had fun when he'd talked her into bar hopping with the kids. For the first time in a long time, he'd felt relaxed and happy, and it had as much to do with being with Claire as it had with spending time with the entire group. But then Diane had called and for some reason, that had set him off. Diane was good at that. She managed to make him angry quite often. Like all the time.

Jim stood slowly, put his hands on his lower back, and bent backward, trying to loosen his tight muscles. He had a lot of apologizing to do tomorrow. But tonight, he had to apologize to the most important person of all. Claire.

Jim walked slowly through the empty street to the lodge. The small village practically rolled up its streets after ten o'clock. This was not a party island, which was part of its charm. There was a lot of drinking, to be sure, but people tended to be back at their hotels at night, or maybe taking a romantic moonlit stroll on the beach. It was a lovely place, and he felt even sorrier for trying to ruin everyone's time tonight.

It was dark inside the room when Jim quietly entered. Claire had left one window curtain pushed aside and moonlight spilled into the room. Across the bed, Claire was curled up under the blankets, facing away from him. She didn't move when he came in. He quietly went into the bathroom and splashed cold water on his face, then readied for bed. When he came out, he saw that Claire still hadn't moved.

Jim sat down on the noisy cot, expecting the creaking sound to evoke a response from Claire. It didn't. Yet, he felt she was still awake. Her breathing was steady, but not the deep breathing of sleep.

"Claire," he said softly. "Are you awake?" When she didn't respond, he continued anyway. "I'm sorry about tonight. I'm sorry about the way I acted and the way I spoke to you. I have no excuse for my behavior. Just because Diane pissed me off, there was no reason for me to take it out on you and everyone else. You're right. I have no right judging you after what I've done to you. I'm sorry, Claire. About all of it. I'm sorry for tonight, for ruining your trip, and most of all, for ruining your life. I never planned it this way. Any of it. Claire? Are you awake?" he stopped and listened, but Claire didn't move or make a sound.

As quietly as he could, Jim slipped into the cot. It creaked and squawked and his back was already feeling the effects of it. "Goodnight, Claire," he said softly into the dark room.

Chapter Eight

When Claire woke up, she was surprised to see that Jim was already gone. She must have slept so soundly that she didn't hear him get up or shower. She was, however, relieved. Maybe it was better that she didn't talk to him this morning. They needed some space.

As Claire showered and dressed, she thought about the words Jim had said to her last night after he'd come back to the room. She'd heard him walk in, but had laid there quietly so she wouldn't have to talk to him. She hadn't trusted herself to speak. Earlier, before he'd come in, she'd cried tears of anger, frustration, and even heartbreak. After four years apart, she'd thought she was completely over her ex-husband. She'd moved on. She now had Steven. Yet, his behavior and his angry words at her last night had hurt her deeply.

When they'd divorced, they'd never had a chance to talk about why he was leaving. He'd just left. For months afterwards, Claire racked her brain wondering what she'd done wrong to make him want to leave her for another woman. Sure, they'd been married a long time, and had dated for two years before that. They knew each other completely. But there had never been any warning signs that he was unhappy with their marriage. None. Zip. Nada. Had she ignored him too much? Had she put the boutique ahead of her marriage? Had she gained too much weight or grown too old that he was no longer attracted to her? Sure, she'd been comfortable in their marriage, but weren't they supposed to be comfortable as the years went by? Claire had never had any answers to her questions, and that had always weighed heavily on her.

Claire had heard every word Jim said last night when he thought she was asleep. He'd told her he was sorry for ruining her life. She couldn't honestly say he'd ruined her life. Yes, she'd had a difficult couple of years after he left worrying about whether the boutique could support her and if she could afford to keep the house that he'd willingly handed over to her. She'd worried about expenses like health insurance since she could no longer be on his and prayed she wouldn't get sick. And she'd worried that maybe she wasn't worth loving, and that she might be alone for the rest of her life. But soon the boutique's income had increased and she found she could afford all her bills, even health insurance. She met Steven, and was relieved that someone found her attractive and interesting again. Yet, even though she was doing very well, it was hard for her not to continue to worry or have anxiety at times. She'd learned that nothing lasts forever and nothing was a sure thing, like she'd thought her marriage to Jim had been. So, it was hard for her to relax completely and let her guard down.

No, Jim hadn't completely ruined her life, but their break up had changed her in ways she hadn't even realized until last night.

Once she was dressed, Claire walked over to the patio window and looked out at the pool area where breakfast was served. She knew Mandy and Craig were already on the early ferry to Marsh Harbour. She saw some of the wedding party down there, eating, and Jim was down there, too. Claire grimaced. She didn't feel like seeing him yet, so she decided to walk uptown to the coffeehouse they'd passed on their way to dinner last night and have something to eat there.

The morning was already heating up to be another

beautiful, tropical day and the breeze off the harbor bay was heavenly. Everyone Claire passed on her walk to the coffeehouse said a cheery hello, and it lightened her mood. It didn't matter that they didn't know her, everyone was friendly here. She loved that. She couldn't have imagined a more charming vacation place than this lovely little island.

On one street corner, tucked away behind flowering hibiscus bushes and squatty palm trees, sat a Victorian home that had been turned into a coffeehouse. Claire walked up the steps and was pleased to see an outside patio with tables that were hidden away from the street. She walked into the building and was immediately tantalized by the aroma of fresh baked goods and creamy coffees. After ordering a huge blueberry muffin and a cappuccino, Claire took it out to a table at the edge of the patio and sat with her back to the entrance. She felt like she was wrapped in a safe cocoon of privacy as she enjoyed her breakfast. She took out her phone and clicked on an app that allowed her to message internationally for free. She began texting Ariana at the shop to find out how things were going.

After a time, Claire noticed Janice and Carl come up the steps and enter the coffeehouse. She sighed. They were really the last people, besides Jim, that she wanted to see. And if she didn't want to seem rude, she'd have to invite them to sit with her. But when they came out with their coffees, they only smiled and nodded at Claire then went to the other end of the patio to sit.

Claire frowned. *What did I do to them?* She decided it was best to leave them alone and continued texting Ariana.

"Do you mind if I sit with you?"

The voice behind Claire startled her. She turned, and there was Jim, a coffee cup in his hand. She was surprised she hadn't heard him come up the stairs. "Geez, I can't seem to get away from you, can I?" Claire said.

"Does that mean no?"

Claire sighed. "Go ahead, sit down," she told him.

"Thank you." Jim sat in the chair next to Claire, which irritated her. She moved her chair a little bit away from his.

"I didn't see you come down for breakfast," Jim said, taking a sip of his coffee.

"That's because I came here instead. After last night, I wasn't too keen on spending time with you this morning."

Jim looked directly at Claire. His eyes looked tired. Sad. "I'm sorry about last night," he said. "You were already asleep when I came into the room, so I'm sure you didn't hear me apologize, but I hope you will accept my apology today. I was a jerk last night, and I have no excuse for my behavior. I'm sorry."

Claire nodded. "Thank you," she said softly. "But I think Mandy, Craig, and the Fishers deserve an apology more than I do."

"Already done," Jim said. "I got up early and caught Mandy and Craig at the ferry dock before they left, then I talked to Janice and Carl at breakfast."

"Well, that's good," Claire said.

Jim tipped his head toward the Fishers sitting across the patio. "What's going on with them?" he asked quietly. "Did you piss them off?"

Claire shook her head. "They just walked past me to their own table," she whispered. "I figured they wanted to be alone."

"Hmmm," was all Jim replied.

Claire's phone buzzed and she looked down at the text that had come through. She started texting back.

Jim cocked his head. "Who are you texting?"

"Ariana. At the shop."

"I thought you said calls and texts were expensive here," Jim said.

Claire looked up. "Ariana and I both downloaded an app that lets us text back and forth for free. Calls are expensive though."

Jim's eyes twinkled with mischief. "And did you tell Steven about this app?"

Claire bit her lip. "No, I didn't."

"Why not?"

"If you must know, I didn't want to be sent constant reminders that I should be thinking about his proposal. Steven isn't really that much of a texter, but I was afraid he'd bombard me while I was here." Claire looked at Jim with a sly grin. "You can tell Diane about it so she can text you."

Jim raised his hands as if to ward off a blow. "No, thank you," he said.

Claire laughed, which made Jim smile.

"So, what does Ariana have to say?" Jim asked.

"She told me to stop texting her and stop worrying about the shop and just enjoy my vacation."

Jim laughed. "That sounds exactly like her. I always did like her."

From behind them, Jim and Claire heard footsteps and turned to see the Fishers standing beside their table.

"Good morning," Claire said, trying to sound cheery. "Would you like to join us?"

Janice shook her head no, but she did manage a small smile. "We just wanted to let you both know that this afternoon, after Mandy and Craig come back, we're going over to see the lighthouse. Sandra said we can catch the ferry to go over there. We thought you might like to join us."

Claire's mouth almost dropped open in shock, but she managed to keep it shut. "Yes, that sounds nice. What time do you think you'll be going?"

"Somewhere around two-thirty or three. We'll meet you on

the front patio at the lodge," Janice said.

Jim and Claire both said they'd be there and the Fishers left. Claire turned and looked at Jim with her brows raised. "Well, I didn't expect that. It's nice that they're trying to be friendly."

Jim nodded. "It is. Maybe we could take a page from their book and try harder being friendly with each other, too?"

"Hey, I have been friendly. Who allowed you to sleep in her room?" Claire asked.

Jim chuckled. "Yeah. After you said I could sleep out in a hammock for the entire vacation."

Claire grinned. "It sounded like a good idea to me."

"I'll bet it did. Listen, I won't try to make you angry if you won't try to kick me out of the room, okay?" Jim said.

Claire stared at him one long moment. "Okay," she finally answered. "I'll try, but I can't make any promises."

Jim finished the last of his coffee and Claire did, too.

"What are you going to do today?" he asked.

"I was thinking of checking out the gift shops and exploring the island a little," Claire told him. She sat there, debating, then made up her mind. "Do you want to tag along?"

Jim grinned that annoyingly adorable grin. "I was hoping you'd ask so I wouldn't have to invite myself along."

Claire shook her head at him and they both stood and walked down the steps.

The narrow streets weren't exactly packed with people, but they did pass other tourists and locals along the way as they walked to the first gift shop. All the business buildings in town were of wooden design and many looked like homes that had been converted into shops. Claire guessed that most of the owners lived upstairs above their businesses. The painted buildings were a mixture of colors, from pastel, to bright lime greens and hot pinks, making the streets as colorful as the fruity drinks served in the bars around here. Claire loved all the colors and the many flowering plants they passed. Living in Minnesota where flowers only bloomed a few months out of the year, she appreciated seeing so many flowers and lush greenery here.

Claire and Jim walked through the few shops on the small island. In one, they ran into Kaylie and Mark. Both were dressed like they were heading to the beach with Kaylie in a swimsuit with a flowery, short tank dress over it and Mark in a T-shirt and board shorts. Claire liked Mark, even though she didn't know him too well. He was easygoing, had longish brown hair and blue eyes. As a couple, he and Kaylie looked adorable.

Jim found an antique style map of the Bahama Islands at one gift shop and purchased it. He said he was going to frame it for his den at home. The entire time they browsed in the shops, Claire noticed he didn't once look at items for Diane, and wondered why.

Claire found a red print sundress that she thought would be perfect for Ariana, but no matter how hard she searched, she couldn't seem to find a gift for Steven. He was so practical, everything she looked at seemed silly for him. She figured she'd be shopping again before they left and would hopefully find something then.

They were almost to the end of the island when they decided they'd better head back to the lodge. Claire looked up a side street and saw it led to the strip of beach that went all the way to the lodge.

"Are you game for walking the beach back to the lodge?" she asked Jim.

"I am if you are," he said.

They walked up the side street and then went down the steps to the beach. They slipped off their flip flops, headed down to the water, and walked in the direction of the lodge.

"Okay," Jim said. "In the spirit of being nice, I'll stay on safe topics. How is the house holding out?"

Claire smiled. "It's doing fine. I had to replace the pipes around the guest bathroom, because they were old and clogged up. Luckily, the rest of the house's pipes were good, so it wasn't too expensive."

Jim nodded. "Yeah, that house is getting old. It was already twenty years old when we bought it, and we've had it, what, fifteen years now?"

Claire slid her eyes toward Jim. "*We* had it eleven years. *I've* had it four years now. Remember, it's mine since the divorce."

"Oh, yeah. Sorry. Old habit saying *we*. I gave you the house in the settlement, because you deserved it. I mean, since I was the one who left. Boy, did that ever piss off Diane, though."

Claire frowned. "Why? She couldn't have possibly wanted an older home. I heard that you two have a very nice new home. Bigger than mine."

Jim wrinkled his nose. "Oh yeah, it's big and new and full of new furniture. I have the mortgage to prove it. Diane wouldn't have settled for anything less."

Claire glanced over at Jim curiously. It sounded to her like he resented the house, and Diane.

"Will you and Steven live in the house if you get married?" Jim asked.

Claire stopped walking. The question had taken her by surprise. "I'm not sure," she said. "Steven lives in a townhouse. He's always telling me I should sell the house and get a townhouse, too. He says the house is too much upkeep for me all alone."

It was Jim's turn to look surprised. "But you love that house. Would you really sell it to move into a townhouse?"

Claire turned and walked a few steps up to where the sand was dry, then sat down facing the ocean. Jim followed and sat, too.

"I do love my house, that's why I've been resisting the idea of getting something simpler. Steven's right, though. The house is expensive and time consuming to keep up. It's due for a new roof, and I'm always mowing the yard in the summer or have to shovel the driveway in the winter. And the heating costs just keep climbing in the winter. It's expensive for me there alone."

"I guess I hadn't thought of that," Jim said. "It would be a shame to sell it, though. All those memories. Mandy grew up in that house. There's the door frame with her heights marked on it, and those of her friends through the years, too. And the crabapple tree you planted when we first moved in. I'll bet that's huge now. And all the remodeling we did, like tearing out that horrible red carpet in the family room and replacing it. Remember that?"

Claire laughed. "Oh, yes, I remember that awful stuff. And the multicolored carpet in the kitchen circa late 1970s. And the gold burlap wallpaper in the hallway. It was terrible."

Jim laughed along with Claire as they remembered all the changes they'd made to update the house. After a time, they both sat silent.

"I guess things change," Jim finally said. "Time moves on, people move on. It's good, I guess. Sometimes." He sounded wistful to Claire.

Jim finally stood up, wiped the sand off the back of his shorts, and picked up the bag with his map in it and Claire's bag from the gift shop, too. He reached out his hand to help her up. Claire accepted it and Jim pulled her to her feet. For one instant, they stood there, hands linked, looking into each other's blue eyes. Claire was the first to let go.

"Guess we'd better get back to the lodge so we're not late meeting up with everyone," Claire said, wiping the sand from her shorts as Jim had.

They walked down the beach, this time silent, each one keeping their thoughts to themselves.

Chapter Nine

Claire and Jim returned to the lodge in time to put their purchases in their room and change into sneakers for the trip to the lighthouse. Claire wasn't sure how much walking was involved so she thought sneakers were the safe choice. She knew for sure she wasn't climbing up inside the lighthouse. She had a terrifying fear of heights.

They each took their cameras and a bottle of water from the room's small refrigerator and walked down the stairs to the patio. Mandy and Craig were already sitting down there when Claire and Jim arrived.

"Get your license all squared away?" Jim asked.

Mandy smiled. "Yep. We're one step closer to being stuck with each other forever," she said, her eyes twinkling mischievously.

Janice and Carl came through the breezeway from the back of the lodge with Glen and Lisa right behind them.

"Let's go catch the ferry," Glen said. "It should be down there in less than five minutes.

The group hurried down the steps to the street and crossed over to the dock where the ferry stopped. Sure enough, it arrived five minutes later like Glen had said.

"What is the rest of the group doing today?" Claire asked Mandy as soon as they were all seated on the ferry.

"Everyone went down to Land's End beach again today. They'll all be back in time for dinner," Mandy answered.

The ferry driver made two more stops to pick people up at other docks and then headed across the harbor to the lighthouse. Their group was the only one to get off there, and the ferry driver told them he'd be back in about an hour.

The small group made their way in the direction of the lighthouse. They were the only people around. There was a small gift shop off to the right of the walkway, but that was it for buildings except for the lighthouse. As they walked up the sidewalk to the lighthouse, everyone stopped to admire the flowers blooming all around and to take pictures of the lighthouse close up.

Claire told Mandy and Craig to stand with the lighthouse in the background and snapped a picture of them, then asked Janice and Carl to join them for a picture of the foursome. Glen took Claire's camera and snapped a photo of her and Jim with Mandy and Craig, too. Then it was Glen and Lisa's turn to have their photo taken. They were all having fun, even the Fishers.

Once they stepped inside the small lighthouse, Claire stepped aside to let everyone pass by her.

"I'll just wait for all of you down here," she said.

"Mom. Don't you want to go up and see the island from above? I'll bet it's beautiful," Mandy said.

"Honey, you know heights and I don't mix well. Just looking up that spiral staircase makes me dizzy. I'll wait for all of you down here. I can get some good pictures of the island from the dock."

Mandy sighed, but turned and followed Craig up the circular staircase. Janice and Carl followed behind them, then Glen and Lisa. Jim held back.

"I'll bet Mandy's right," Jim said. "The view up there must be incredible. Why don't you just try? If you feel sick, I'll help you come down right away."

Claire shook her head. "Don't you remember how dizzy I got when we climbed that fire tower years ago when Mandy was little? Or the time we went to the Grand Canyon and I practically passed out trying to look over the railing? There's no way I'm going to repeat that."

"You fly. That doesn't bother you," Jim said.

"That's because I don't sit by the window and I'm inside a plane. It's not the same as climbing stairs or looking down a canyon. I know I'll get sick. Or worse, I'll get up there and won't be able to come down," Claire said.

Jim shook his head. "You're going to miss out."

"Stop goading me," Claire said menacingly.

"But it's a once in a lifetime experience," Jim said.

"What happened to being nice to each other?"

Jim smiled. "I am being nice. I don't want you to miss it. Listen, I'll walk up right behind you to make sure you don't fall and then help you down again. Come on, Claire. You know you want to go up there."

Claire looked up at the spiral staircase, then back at Jim. He was right, she did really want to go up and see the view. But just looking up made her queasy. Yet, she was never going to be here again, and she'd love to have great pictures from above.

"Okay," she told Jim. "I'll go up. But I swear, if I get sick, I'm going to throw up all over you for making me go."

"Well, it won't be the first time, now will it?" he teased.

Claire threw him a nasty look.

Claire hung her camera around her neck to free her hands. With Jim right behind her, Claire started ascending the staircase, holding the railings with both hands. Going up the first few turns wasn't so bad as long as she didn't look down. But the higher they went, the narrower the steps became, and Claire had to look down to see the steps. She stopped once when she saw the ground far below and she started to waver. Jim reached up with one hand and put it on her waist to steady her.

"Easy there. Try not to look down. You're doing fine," he told her.

Near the top, Claire stopped and glanced up in fear. The last few steps up to the very top weren't really steps at all. It was a ladder built into the wall that went up through an opening in the floor of the top landing.

"Oh, boy. I don't think I can do this," she said fearfully.

"Yes, you can," Jim told her in a soothing voice. "Go ahead, I'm right behind you."

Claire reached for the railings, grabbed on tight, and put her foot on the first step. She pulled herself up to the second step. Then the third. She felt Jim right behind her, just one step below her. If she let go, they'd both go tumbling down to the platform. That thought scared her half to death.

"I can do this, I can do this," Claire chanted quietly to herself.

Jim smiled behind her. "Just keep saying that, Claire."

Claire looked up and saw Glen standing near the opening, ready to help her. She felt a little better. Three more steps and her head was through the hole in the floor. Two more steps and Glen took her hands and helped her up and onto the floor.

"There you go, Little Sis," Glen said.

They stepped aside to let Jim through.

"See, you made it," Jim said triumphantly.

Claire smiled, but then looked down the hole she'd come up through. She wasn't looking forward to climbing down.

"Mom, you came up," Mandy exclaimed happily. "Come over here. You can circle the entire floor and see everything for miles around."

Claire let go of Glen, who she'd been hanging on tightly to since he'd helped her up. She followed Mandy to the small windows that lined the walls in a complete circle. The room was small, almost claustrophobic. Claire hoped she could look out the windows without passing out.

Slowly, Claire edged her way to the window next to Mandy. She peered out. Mandy and Jim had been right. It was an amazing view of the island and beyond.

Jim came up behind Claire and looked over her shoulder. "Aren't you happy that you didn't miss this?" he asked.

Claire nodded. She started taking pictures of the island from every view, moving from window to window, with Jim protectively following her. The ocean beyond the island was a beautiful variation of blues and greens that went on forever into the bright blue horizon. Claire snapped picture after picture, enjoying the lovely scenery.

Soon, Janice, Carl, Mandy, and Craig left the room and headed down the stairway. Glen helped Lisa through the opening in the floor, then asked Claire if she'd like him to stay and help her down.

"No, you go ahead. I want to take a few more pictures before we go down," Claire said. She felt confident now since the view wasn't making her queasy. Glen disappeared down the stairs.

After Claire and Jim had taken as many photos as they wanted, it was time to go down. All the giddiness Claire had felt about being able to look out the windows without getting sick disappeared when she looked down the opening to the ladder. Fear began to rise inside her and she felt the color drain from her face.

"Are you okay?" Jim asked.

"I'm not sure. How am I going to get through that hole and grab ahold of the ladder without falling through?" Claire asked, starting to panic.

"I can hold your hand to steady you while you step down," Jim said.

Claire eyes grew wide. "But then who will help me down from below if you are up here and I'm on the ladder? What if I fall? Oh, my God. I should have told Glen to stay. I can't do this with just your help."

Jim grasped both of Claire's arms, making her focus on him. "Okay, steady now. Don't panic. You can do this. I'll go through first, then you can come down after me, okay? I'll grab you if you lose your balance."

Claire looked into Jim's eyes. She had to trust him. She had to believe she could get down from here. There was no alternative. She couldn't stay up here forever.

"Ready?" Jim asked.

Claire slowly nodded.

Jim walked over to the opening, turned around, grabbed the railings, and stepped down onto the first step. "See how I did it?" he asked Claire. "You do it the same way, okay?"

Claire nodded. She watched Jim step down another step, then another, until there was room for her to step down. She walked over to the opening and looked down at Jim. She felt dizzy. Claire closed her eyes tight.

"I can't do this," she told Jim, backing away. "I can't. I'll fall. I'll knock you down. I can't do this."

"Claire, listen to me," Jim said calmly. "You can do this. Just come over here and don't look down. Grab the railing tight, then step down onto the first step. I'm right here. I won't let you fall."

Claire felt like crying. Tears welled up in her eyes. *I shouldn't have come up here. I'm never going to be able to get down.*

"Claire. It's okay. Everything's going to be okay. You can do this. Come on. You can do this."

Jim's soothing voice kept urging her forward. Claire finally opened her eyes, swiped the tears away, and inched toward the opening. She turned around and grabbed tightly to the railings.

Hanging on for dear life, she slowly reached one foot down toward the ladder's step. She hesitated, not sure where it was, then she felt a warm hand on her ankle, guiding her foot to the step. Through her sneaker, she finally felt the step, and placed her weight on it.

"There you go," Jim said. "Now, keep hanging on tight and move your other foot through and onto the next step."

Claire did as she was told. Again, she felt Jim's hand on her ankle to guide her foot to the step. She let out a sigh of relief.

"Now just keep coming down the ladder," Jim told her. "I'm right here. Right behind you."

Slowly, Claire moved her right foot, then her left foot, finding the next ladder step for each one. She felt calmer with each step she went down. Finally, she heard Jim step onto the landing where the actual stairway started, and she stepped one foot down on it, too. She felt Jim's hands circle her waist as she slowly dropped her other foot onto the landing. She opened her eyes to see where she was and accidently looked down the middle of the stairway to the bottom floor where everyone else was waiting for them. Claire wavered, feeling dizzy again.

"It's okay, Claire," Jim said softly into her ear. "I've got you. I'm not going to let you go."

Claire closed her eyes and stood there a moment until she felt steadier on her feet. Feeling Jim's hands on her waist made her feel safer. Much safer.

"Ready to go the rest of the way?" Jim asked.

Claire nodded. They walked to the staircase with Jim's arm around her waist, steadying her. Slowly, step by step, they walked down the staircase together with Claire hanging onto the handrail with one hand, and the other hand grasping Jim's waist. Jim held her tightly against him, never letting go.

The others were already outside when Jim and Claire made it to the bottom step. Claire still clung to Jim, even after they were on the main floor.

"Are you okay?" he whispered to her.

"Yeah. I just need to get my bearings," she said, standing there. "Sorry I was so much trouble, but you already knew I was afraid of heights."

"No trouble at all," he said softly, looking directly at Claire. Jim leaned over and placed a soft kiss on her cheek. "Happy to do it." He slowly pulled away and walked out into the bright daylight.

Claire stood there a moment, thinking about what had just happened. She reached her hand up to her cheek and touched it where Jim had just kissed her. Regaining her balance and her composure, she followed him outside into the sunlight.

That night the entire wedding group ate dinner at The Red Snapper Inn on the other side of the island. They'd all dressed up and driven their golf carts there. Janice and Carl had ridden with Mandy and Craig, and Claire had ridden with Jim. It was another beautiful evening with a clear sky and warm air.

The Red Snapper Inn was one of the three resorts on the island and also boasted an upscale restaurant. They sat at a long table on the enclosed patio that had large windows all around. Like every place on the island, there was a spectacular view of the ocean.

The food was delicious. Everyone had ordered some type of seafood, except for the Fishers who had stuck with chicken again. Claire had tried the local lobster that came with delicious roasted red potatoes and asparagus tips. Jim had tried the fish of the day, steamed grouper, and shared a bite with Claire.

"Is the food better tasting here on the island?" Claire asked everyone at the table. "Or does it just seem better tasting, because there is always such a great view?"

Everyone in the group laughed, but agreed that everything they'd eaten since coming to the island had been delicious.

Night fell as they finished dinner. Claire and Jim had shared a slice of cheesecake with strawberries on it, and Claire felt like she was going to burst from eating so much food. Mandy and Craig suggested taking a walk on the beach before driving back to the resort, and everyone agreed that would be nice. Janice and Carl stayed behind, though, and waited for them in the bar.

Mandy grabbed her mother's arm and they walked ahead of the group. "You and Dad seem to be doing okay today," she said.

Claire nodded. "Yeah. He's been behaving himself since last night."

Mandy rolled her eyes. "Last night was awful. But he apologized to us this morning. What set off his bad mood?"

"Diane," Claire said. "She was mad at him about a picture you'd posted on Facebook. We were in it, and he was rubbing suntan lotion on my back. She blew a gasket over it."

Mandy turned toward her mother, her hand raised to her mouth. "Oh, no. I didn't mean to start anything by posting pictures. I posted pictures of the scenery. I didn't even notice you and Dad in the picture. Should I take it down?"

A small smile appeared on Claire's face. She wasn't usually a mean-spirited person, but she did enjoy making Diane angry. "Ah, just leave it up. It's your Facebook page. You can have whatever you want on it."

Mandy shot her mother a sideways glance. "You just want to piss off Diane, don't you?"

Claire looked at her daughter with a fake shocked expression. "Who, me? Never."

Both women laughed.

"Can you imagine what she'd do if she knew you and Daddy were sharing a room?" Mandy asked.

"Hmmm. Maybe you should post that to Facebook, too,"

Claire said, waggling her eyebrows.

"You can be really evil, you know that?" Mandy said, giggling. "I don't want to upset Dad's wife that much. After all, he has to live with her."

Claire agreed. After how nice Jim had been to her today at the lighthouse, she really didn't want to do anything to upset his wife, or life, either.

Mandy fell back to walk with Craig and soon all the couples paired off and walked down the beach. That left Claire and Jim together again. Claire didn't mind tonight. At least they were getting along well, and it was such a beautiful evening, it was nice sharing it with someone.

"You know what this reminds me of?" Jim asked Claire as they walked side-by-side at the water's edge.

"What?"

"When we were in college and a group of us would go to the lake for the day and hang out on the beach. Remember? We'd usually stay late into the evening and start a bonfire. Those were the days, huh? When we had nothing more to worry about except getting to class on time and having fun."

Claire looked up at him, surprised he'd brought up the old days. They'd met in her first year of college in an economics class. Jim had been one year ahead of her. Both had majored in Business Management, so they often had the same classes together. They started dating seriously in her sophomore year. Then, in her junior year, Claire discovered she was pregnant with Mandy and she and Jim were married that summer. Luckily, he'd already graduated college. Claire never finished her last year. Now, it seemed like such a long time ago. Almost like another lifetime.

"Yeah. Those were the days," Claire agreed. "But real life is always more complicated than college life. Ours grew complicated before we even finished college."

Jim glanced up to where Mandy walked with Craig, then back at Claire. "Maybe," he said. "But I wouldn't have traded having Mandy for anything else in the world."

Claire's heart swelled. It was nice hearing that he'd at least been happy they'd married and had Mandy, even though their marriage hadn't lasted in the end.

The air grew chilly and the group turned back toward the inn to collect Janice and Carl and drove the golf carts to the lodge. Everyone said goodnight and headed to their rooms. Before leaving, Mandy told her parents that she and Craig were going down to the top of the dune by the beach to lay down and look up at the night sky. "You should try it," she told Jim and Claire. "It's so peaceful and beautiful."

"Maybe another night," Claire said. She hugged her daughter goodnight.

"Nothing like being young and in love," Jim said wistfully as he watched Mandy and Craig walk away hand in hand.

Claire nodded. "Yeah. Hopefully it will last for them."

Jim turned to Claire and looked at her tenderly. "Our marriage wasn't so bad, was it? I mean, until I screwed everything up."

Claire didn't know how to answer him. She had thought they had a good marriage, but then he'd left her and she still didn't understand why.

"Something must have been wrong," she said sadly. "Otherwise, we'd still be together."

Jim sighed. "I guess that was a stupid question, huh? But I believe our marriage was a good one, even with the way things turned out."

Claire turned away from Jim, afraid that if she stayed close to him, her emotions would bubble up to the surface. This was no time for tears. She silently agreed, their marriage had been good. That was why his leaving had been such a shock.

"Okay. No more stupid questions," Jim said, the lightness now back in his voice. "It's late. Let's go up to bed."

Claire and Jim walked up the three flights of stairs to their room. For one fleeting moment, Claire wished things had been different and they were still together. But now there were other people involved, and that wish could no longer come true.

* * *

Jim lay awake in his uncomfortable cot long after they'd turned out the lights and Claire had fallen asleep. The moonlight filtered through an opening in the curtains over the patio door, and Jim heard the sound of the ocean waves in the distance. Claire had left the patio door open a crack again tonight so they'd be lulled to sleep by the sound of the ocean. Unfortunately, it hadn't helped him fall asleep so easily.

Jim thought back through their day together, and it made him smile. He'd been such a jerk the night before because of Diane's phone call, but Claire had been kind enough to understand and forgive him. That was the Claire he remembered. The kind, caring woman who had always stood by him, encouraged him, and most of all, trusted him. The fact that she'd still be so nice to him after he'd broken that trust four years ago made him feel even more remorseful now. And he'd felt terrible, no downright dreadful, when he'd left her.

Jim thought back to the day he'd left, and, for the life of him, he couldn't think of one good reason why he'd done it. Claire had never been a nagger. She'd never asked more of him than she'd given of herself. She'd been the perfect mother, and had never once made Jim feel as if he came second in their marriage. Yet, he'd still cheated and he'd still left her. Why?

"Something must have been wrong, otherwise, we'd still be together," Claire had said to him tonight. He hadn't known how to

respond when she'd said it because, if he were honest with himself, he knew that there had been nothing wrong with their relationship. There had only been something wrong with him.

Jim turned in the cot to try to get more comfortable and was rewarded with a loud creaking noise. He lay still for a moment, listening, until he decided that he hadn't awoken Claire. The cot was a torture device, and maybe the fact that he was stuck on it was well-deserved. It was just one of the universe's ways of exacting revenge on him for hurting Claire. Another form of revenge had been living with Diane. If the universe hadn't been laughing at him for being stuck with her after having had Claire, he'd be surprised. Karma was a bitch, and so was Diane.

Jim pushed away all thoughts of the horrible cot and of his soon-to-be ex-wife and thought about the lovely day he and Claire had shared. It had felt so good to enjoy an easy-going day exploring the gift shops and walking the beach. Helping Claire with her fear of heights at the lighthouse had been unexpected, but nice. Even though she'd been afraid, he'd been able to help her see the view from above, and he knew she'd be pleased with the photos she'd taken. It had also felt good being needed by her. He'd come to her aid when she'd needed him, and he'd followed through. At least this time he hadn't abandoned her when she'd needed him most.

Jim had also noticed that Claire hadn't been as nervous today as she'd been the first few days of the trip. She hadn't spun her charm bracelet around her wrist or twirled her necklace endlessly. That meant she'd been relaxed and enjoyed her day, too. Or, at least he hoped it meant that.

Jim hoped that the rest of the vacation went as nicely as today had. For a fleeting instant, he wondered if he should tell Claire that he and Diane were through. Would that make a difference to her? Would it help her decide if she really wanted to marry that stuck-up Steven, or not? He didn't know for sure how she'd react to the news. Would it help to bring him and Claire closer? Or would it matter at all to Claire. A little part of him wished it would matter.

When Jim finally fell asleep, it was to the lulling sound of the waves, but also to the light, steady breathing of the first love of his life, and perhaps, the only love of his life, sleeping only a few feet away from him.

Chapter Ten

Claire awoke the next morning to the sun peeking through the partially closed curtains. She reached over, pulled one curtain aside, and hooked it open, then lay back and sighed. The view outside the window was glorious. It was another sunny day with blue skies and puffy white clouds overhead.

Claire picked up her phone and unlocked it to see what time it was. Nine-thirty a.m. Wow, she hadn't realized she'd slept so late, but it had felt good. She couldn't remember when she'd slept in this late in a long time.

Claire felt something move beside her, and she turned to see Jim smiling back at her. She jumped, startled by his nearness. "What on earth are you doing in my bed?" she exclaimed, pulling the blankets tighter around her. "You scared the bejeezus out of me."

"Sorry," Jim said sheepishly. "I didn't mean to scare you. And technically, I'm not *in* your bed, I'm *on* your bed. See? I'm on top of the comforter and you're safely tucked under the blankets. No one is touching anyone."

Claire rolled her eyes and fell back on her pillows. "That's not the point. You're on *my* bed, uninvited. How long have you been there?"

"I'm sorry," Jim repeated. "But that cot is killing me. Plus, it was making so much noise, I was afraid I'd wake you."

Claire stared hard at Jim. "How long?"

"Only an hour or so."

Claire sighed, then lifted her arms in surrender. "I feel like I've lost control of everything. First my room, now my bed. Is there anything else in my life you'd like to take?"

Jim grinned and leaned over closer to her. "Well, if you're offering…" he started to say, but Claire cut him off.

"No, I'm not," she said pointedly. "I'm going to shower and then head over to that delightful coffeehouse and have one of their delicious muffins and a coffee. What are you doing this morning?"

Jim continued smiling that rakish grin of his as he watched Claire pull clean clothes out of her suitcase and walk toward the bathroom. "I'll go anywhere you're going," he said.

Claire shook her head and escaped into the bathroom, but there was a small smile on her face.

Later, Claire sat at a table on the patio of the coffeehouse while Jim went inside to order their coffee and food. She was surprised when her phone buzzed in her pocket. When she pulled it out and looked at it, she sighed. Steven. He probably wanted to know if she was still thinking about his proposal. In truth, she'd stopped thinking about it the past two days and was just enjoying her vacation. But she didn't dare tell him that. It would hurt his feelings.

Reluctantly, she answered the phone. "Hi, Steven."

"Hello, Claire. How is everything going there?"

Claire frowned. Steven sounded very happy. Almost jovial. She was used to him being more serious. "Everything is fine. How about you?"

"Couldn't be better. In fact, it's been pretty amazing here. The staff has sold more houses this week than we sold all last month. It's incredible."

"That's wonderful," Claire said, genuinely happy for him. "Congratulations."

"Thanks. But that isn't why I called. Have you thought any

more about us getting married?" Steven asked, his tone turning serious.

Claire bit her lip. "Of course, I have," she lied. "I'd really rather talk about our future when I get back, though."

"I understand completely," Steven said. "The thing is, well, I was thinking that even if you decide that you aren't ready to get married, I'd like you to consider moving in together."

Claire's mouth dropped open. She hadn't expected this turn of events. "Move in together?"

"Of course," Steven said. "We've been dating over two years and we're very compatible. I think it's time we move forward, even if you decide not to marry me yet. I mean, it's really just a matter of time that we will get married once you get used to the idea. And there's no sense of us both having to maintain a home. What do you think?"

Claire didn't know what to think. This seemed so sudden to her. "Well… first of all, where would we live? Your place? My house?"

"I was thinking my place," Steven said. "It's much easier to maintain, and there's plenty of room for the both of us. We'd have everything here at the complex. There's the workout room, the pool, and the golf course is just a few steps away. It would be perfect."

Claire frowned. *Perfect for who? I don't even like to golf.* As she sat there, trying to think of a response, Jim came out with their order on a tray. He raised his brows and nodded to the phone. Claire mouthed that it was Steven, and Jim nodded.

"I'm not sure this is something we need to decide right now," Claire finally said into the phone. "Let's talk about this when I get back. Okay?"

"Well, that's the crazy thing," Steven said. "You see, I have this couple who've been looking for a home for months, and when I told them that your home might be on the market soon, they were really interested. They love the neighborhood and the size is perfect for their family."

Claire had just raised her coffee to her lips for a little caffeine jolt when Steven's words hit her. She was so shocked, she almost dropped her cup. "You did what?"

"I know it sounds a bit out there, but you know how we've talked about you selling your house, and here is an opportunity for you to do just that. I drove the couple by the house and they love it. Think of it. You could sell your house right now and we can move in together. What could be more perfect?"

"What's going on?" Jim whispered, taking a bite of his muffin.

Claire waved his question away. *Was Steven crazy? Sell her house? Right now?* "I'm not ready to sell my house, Steven," Claire said pointedly. "*We* haven't talked about selling my house. *You've* talked about it. I've never said I wanted to sell it. And I'm not even sure I want to move in with you yet."

"He's selling your house?" Jim asked, loudly this time. "Why the hell is he selling the house?"

Claire looked over at Jim. "He's not selling the house. He's just talking about it."

"Who's that with you?" Steven asked. "Is that Jim?"

"Yes, it's Jim. We're having breakfast," Claire said.

"Together? I thought you couldn't stand the sight of him. Where's Diane? Is she eating with you, too?" Steven asked, sounding concerned.

"No. Diane isn't eating with us. She didn't come on the trip. And yes, I'm eating breakfast with Jim. It's a small island. I couldn't ignore him if I tried."

Jim frowned. "Geez, thanks."

Claire made a face and waved at him to shut up.

"Oh," Steven said, his tone changing to his business voice. "Well, maybe I should let you get back to your breakfast."

Claire sighed. *Really? He was jealous?* "Listen, Steven. It's just breakfast. The whole group has been doing almost everything together while we've been here. As for selling my house, I'm not ready to yet. It's not for sale, okay? I'd really rather talk about all this face to face and not during a phone call that's costing me two-fifty a minute."

"You're missing a really good opportunity to sell your home," Steven said. "The perfect buyer doesn't always come around so quickly."

"I'll take my chances," Claire said.

There was a long pause, then Steven finally spoke. "Okay. We'll talk when you get back. Goodbye."

"Bye," Claire said, but she could tell that Steven had already clicked off his phone. Angrily, she turned off her phone.

"What the hell?" Jim asked, looking over at Claire.

"He practically had my house sold and me moving in with him," Claire said, anger rising in her voice. "He even took the people past the house to see it. Can you believe that? Does he really think just because he wants to put a ring on me that he's going to own me?"

Jim whistled low. "Wow. That takes nerve."

"I don't want a man with nerve. I want a man who listens to me and doesn't try to con me. God, what was he thinking? Am I just a commission to him? Who the hell is he to tell me what I want?" Claire grew angrier by the second. She grabbed her charm bracelet and started twirling it around her wrist. "Why do all men think they can manipulate me like that? Am I that much of a pushover? Doesn't anyone think I have a brain of my own?"

Jim reached over and gently placed his hand over hers to stop her from twirling the bracelet. Claire glared at him. Before she could tell him to leave her alone, he caught her eyes with his. "I don't think you're a pushover and I know for sure that you have a brain. You're smart, Claire. You always have been. You raised an intelligent, strong, confident daughter and grew a business out of nothing. Woe to any man who doesn't appreciate you for the capable woman that you are."

Claire slowly pulled her hand away. "Do you really mean that?"

Jim nodded. "With all my heart. I may have been stupid enough to lose you, but I never discounted how amazing you are. Don't let Steven run over you. You deserve better."

Claire took a breath, and surprisingly, felt better from Jim's words. She ate a bite of her muffin and then sipped her coffee. Her anger had subsided. All that was left was disappointment in Steven.

"You know, that really isn't like Steven to be so pushy. He's usually very considerate of my feelings. I can't imagine what got into him," Claire said, feeling she had to defend Steven even after what he'd done.

"Well, he is a salesman," Jim said.

Claire frowned. She hated to admit it, but Jim was right.

From behind them, Claire and Jim heard footsteps and turned to see Mandy coming up the steps to the patio.

"There you two are," Mandy said. "I've been looking all over for you."

"What's going on?" Claire asked as Mandy sat down at their table.

"Everyone is heading down to Land's End beach for the afternoon," Mandy said excitedly. "There's a guy there who's taking people out parasailing, so we all want to try it. I figured you two would want to come, too."

"Parasailing?" Claire asked. "What's that?"

"The guy hooks you up to a parachute and pulls you along with a speedboat until you're flying up high. It looks like fun."

"Are you crazy?" Claire asked. "Being pulled behind a boat with a parachute? Count me out."

"Aw, come on, Claire," Jim said. "It sounds like fun. We could at least go and watch. We can take pictures of the others doing it."

Claire eyed Jim. She didn't trust him not to sign her up for this craziness. "Okay. I'll go to watch, but I won't do it. Understand?"

"Of course," Jim said, winking at Mandy, who smiled back conspiratorially.

Claire narrowed her eyes at both of them. "Understand?" she repeated.

"Oh, Mom. You're so suspicious. Of course we won't make you do it."

Claire didn't trust either of them, but she agreed to go nonetheless.

After Claire changed into shorts and a tank top with a swimsuit underneath and Jim changed into his swim trunks, they joined the group down by the golf carts and drove to the other end of the island. It was another beautiful, sunny day with temperatures in the eighties, and the breeze from riding in the open golf cart felt good. Claire planned on working on her suntan while watching the younger people go up parasailing. Janice and Carl had stayed back at the lodge, and for once, Claire thought they might be the smart ones.

When they arrived at the beach, there were only a few people from a nearby resort signed up for parasailing, so everyone in their group who wanted to parasail signed up on the sheet and waited their turn. Each ride lasted fifteen minutes, and the parasail held two people, so it wasn't long before it was Mandy and Craig's turn to go up.

Claire watched as Mandy and Craig each stepped into the swing-type harness attached to the parachute. They were also given life jackets for safety. The couple was told to stand on the back of the boat and as it gained speed, they would slowly lift off and one of the crewmen would unreel the line that tethered them to the boat. They could go up to five-hundred feet into the sky. Just the thought of being up that high made Claire queasy.

"Are you sure this is safe?" she asked Jim, who stood beside her, taking pictures.

"Of course, it is," he said, grinning. "You saw the other groups go up and come down safely. They'll be fine."

Claire bit her lip. She didn't care if the others came down safely. She only cared if her baby girl was safe.

Everyone watched as Mandy and Craig slowly lifted off the back of the boat as it sped faster across the calm ocean. The parasailing group had explained that they only operated on his side of the island, because the surf was always calmer there. Soon, Mandy and Craig were high up in the sky. They waved at their friends down below and seemed to be having a great time.

"Looks like a blast, huh?" Glen said as he and Lisa came over to stand beside Claire and Jim.

"Looks dangerous to me," Claire said. "Are you two going up?"

"Of course. Wouldn't miss this for anything. The view up there must be amazing," Glen told her.

"You're both crazy," Claire said.

Glen laughed. "You know I am, baby sister." He turned to Jim. "Man, you have to try to talk Claire into going up. She'll love it once she's up there."

Claire glared at Glen. "Are you insane? After what happened at the lighthouse? I almost ended up living up there. No way am I going up in a parachute over the ocean."

Glen shrugged. "Yeah, but you survived the lighthouse, didn't you?"

"Barely," Claire said.

"It would be fun," Jim admitted. "Look at how happy Mandy and Craig are up there. And you can go up in twos. We could go up together."

Claire shook her head. No way was she going to be pulled behind a speedboat as she flew up in the sky.

Soon, everyone took a turn parasailing and each couple came down telling Claire how much fun they had.

"You have to try it, Mom," Mandy told Claire. "It's so amazing. It's like swinging up in Heaven."

"Claire, you have to go up," Lisa told her after she and Glen had their turn. "It feels completely safe and it feels like you're flying. You just can't miss this."

Claire sighed when Kaylie came over to tell her what she was missing out on. Everyone was trying to sell her on parasailing, but she wasn't buying. Just watching them scared her to death. But when the last group went up, Claire noticed Jim watching them with longing in his eyes.

"You should go up," she told him. "Don't miss out because of me."

"No, it's okay. They only have the two-man harness with them today. It's two people or nothing. I admit, it looks like a lot of fun, but I don't have to do it," Jim said.

Claire frowned. She didn't want to ruin Jim's chance of having fun. "Why don't you go up with Mandy? I'm sure she'll be happy to go up again."

Jim shook his head. "I'd rather go up with you. I know you're afraid of heights, but I don't really think this will scare you once you're up there. And they pull you in so smoothly that you never have to touch the water. But I don't want to force you into anything."

Claire felt torn as she watched Cameron and Angela soaring up high. After watching everyone else, she felt tempted to try it. And she also wanted to go up so Jim could go. But part of her was paralyzed with the fear of being up so high. She thought about how much she'd enjoyed the view at the top of the lighthouse. She'd have missed it if Jim hadn't helped her go up there. He'd been so nice, helping her down even though she was panicking. She didn't want Jim to miss out on parasailing just because she was chicken.

Claire closed her eyes, took a deep breath, and blurted out, "Okay. Go sign us up."

Jim turned and looked at her, astounded. "What?"

"I want to go up," Claire said, trying to sound sincere. "Go sign us up to be next."

Jim cocked his head and stared at her. "Are you sure? I don't want you to feel like you have to go up because of me."

Claire managed a small smile. "I'm sure. Let's do this."

When Cameron and Angela came down, Claire and Jim were on the dock, waiting. Mandy stood by her mother, and Glen and Lisa were there, too.

"Are you sure, Mom?" Mandy asked. "You really want to do this?"

Claire took in a deep breath. "Yes, I'm sure. Everyone looked like they were having fun. I'm sure I will, too." *If I don't die of fear first.*

A crewman helped Claire into the harness and snapped it firmly around her waist. He then gave her a life jacket to put on and helped her fit it properly. Jim was harnessed in and had his life jacket on, too. Their harnesses were secured to straps that were attached to a long, padded bar that would be above their heads. The bar was secured to the parachute. Claire was fine up until the moment everything was ready to go and she and Jim were standing on the back of the boat.

"Ready?" the boat driver asked.

Jim nodded. Claire stood there, holding her harness straps

tightly, gritting her teeth.

The boat took off. "It's going to be fine," Jim whispered in Claire's ear. Just breathe."

Easier said than done. Claire squeezed her eyes shut.

As the boat sped faster, Claire felt herself being lifted off the boat. Slowly, inch by inch, she was lifted up higher into the air. She kept her eyes shut, afraid to look down. The wind blew in her face. She was happy she'd kept her sunglasses on so her eyes didn't water. She didn't move. She was afraid if she moved even a little, she'd fall to her death into the ocean.

"I can do this. I can do this. I can do this," Claire chanted softly to herself.

Finally, when it felt as if they were moving at a steady speed, Jim put his mouth to her ear. "Open your eyes, Claire. Look. It's beautiful."

Slowly, Claire inched her eyes open. She looked all around her. There was nothing but blue-green water all around far below her. Her hands grasped the harness straps so tightly, her knuckles turned white. *I'm going to die. I'm going to die.*

"Claire," Jim yelled over the sound of the wind. "Look over there. It's the island." He took one hand off the harness strap and pointed.

Claire's stomach lurched. *Hang on, you idiot,* she wanted to yell, but she couldn't get the words out. She turned her head slowly, and that's when she saw the island. Their group was down there, waving at them. They were so far down, they looked like little, tiny dolls to Claire.

As they continued moving steadily, Claire relaxed. They weren't bumping around, and she started feeling safe in the harness. She looked all around her, and the beauty of her surroundings completely astounded her. She was doing it. She was way up high in the sky, she had her eyes open, and she was actually enjoying the ride. Like a child at an amusement park, she turned to Jim with a huge smile.

"I'm doing it!" she exclaimed with pure joy. "I'm actually up here. I can't believe it!"

Jim smiled back at her. "You are. I'm so proud of you," he said. Then he leaned over and kissed her on the cheek, just like he'd done in the lighthouse. Claire smiled wider.

Claire felt like she was flying. It was an amazing feeling. She realized that she'd never had tried this if it hadn't been for Jim. If she'd been with Steven, he'd have never even wanted to try this. He'd also have never persuaded her to go up in the lighthouse. Jim had always been the one to get her to try things she feared. He'd been the one to hold onto her tightly years ago at the Grand Canyon so she could look over the edge and see the view. He knew, even though she was frightened, she'd want to see down the canyon. And she'd always trusted him to keep her safe. Surprisingly, she still did.

The ride was over sooner than Claire had wanted it to be and they were landing on the back of the boat. One of the crewmen grabbed Claire's hand while another grasped Jim and two others seized the parachute to pull it in quickly. The men worked like clockwork and before Claire knew it, she was out of the harness and life jacket and safely back on the dock with her family and friends.

"Mom. You did it!" Mandy exclaimed, hugging Claire tightly.

Claire smiled. "I did. It was amazing. I'm so happy I went." She turned to Jim. "I'd have never tried to go up if it hadn't been for you," she told him.

Jim smiled and winked at her.

The group started walking toward the golf carts to drive back to the lodge. Jim picked up Claire's beach bag, slung it over his shoulder, and they walked together back to their cart.

Chapter Eleven

That evening, the group went to the Lighthouse View Restaurant for a casual dinner. Tomorrow night, the night before the wedding on Saturday, Janice and Carl were hosting a groom's dinner at the Harbour View Lodge restaurant where they were sure to enjoy an excellent meal. Tonight, they satisfied their hunger with good old fashioned burgers, fries, and other local favorites like fried shrimp and conch.

The atmosphere was festive and special island drinks flowed freely. They had all learned from bar hopping around the island that each bar had their own special concoctions, and everyone wanted to try them. Jim talked Claire into trying a sip of each new drink he had, including a Mudslide, a chocolaty-Kahlua drink, a Sex on the Beach, and a Bushwhacker—Claire didn't even want to know what was in that. Mandy talked Claire into tasting her mango Daiquiri, and Kaylie said she just had to try her Pineapple Daiquiri, too. Being the lightweight Claire was when it came to alcohol, every sip of these strong drinks made her feel a little tipsier.

The moon was up and the night sky was clear when the group walked back to the lodge. Everyone split off when they got there. Janice and Carl headed up to their second-floor room while Kaylie and Mark went out to the dock on the harbor to sit a while. Mandy and Craig said goodnight and strolled hand in hand through the breezeway to their cottage. Glen and Lisa did the same. Soon, Claire and Jim were alone on the patio, looking up at the clear night sky.

"It's too beautiful of a night to just go up to the room," Jim said. "Let's go to the beach and look up at the stars like Mandy suggested the other night."

Claire looked down at the sundress she wore. She wasn't really dressed to be climbing around on a dune, but she was still in an adventurous mood from her exciting day and all the alcohol she'd consumed.

"Sure. Why not?" she said to Jim with a smile. They linked arms and walked through the breezeway and down the walkway to the pool area. The area was still lit up, but the bar was closed for the night and there was no one around.

Instead of walking down the wooden steps to the beach, they walked a short way to the hill that overlooked the beach, stepped through some prickly bushes, and carefully made their way to the top of the dune that ran along the hillside. They found a good spot and Jim held Claire's hand as she slipped off her sandals and sat down. Making sure her dress was smoothed down, Claire lay down on the sand and gazed up into the night sky. Jim lay down beside her.

"Oh, my goodness. Mandy was right. The stars are beautiful," Claire said.

They both lay there, admiring the bright, twinkling stars in the inky black sky as the waves below lapped gently on the beach.

"Look. I see the Little Dipper," Jim said, pointing up to the sky. "Do you see it?"

Claire looked where Jim pointed. "Yes. There it is. What else do you see? I can never find anything in the stars."

Jim smiled. "See over there? That's the Big Dipper."

"Where?"

"Right there," Jim said, pointing again. "Below the Little Dipper and to the left."

Claire searched the stars until she was able to make it out. "I see it," she said, excitedly. "What else?"

Jim searched. Finally, he pointed out another constellation. "If you look almost straight down from the Little Dipper, you can see Orion's Belt. And if you look really close, you'll see all of Orion, even his bow and arrow."

Claire searched, but no matter how hard she tried, she couldn't see Orion. "I think you're making this up. I can't see it."

Jim chuckled. He lifted Claire's hand and pointed it up to the sky. "There, see? There are one, two, three stars for his belt. Below that are two stars farther apart for the bottom of his dress, and above the belt is the outline of his neck and the front of his dress."

Claire giggled. "Orion wears a dress?"

"Whatever they called it in those days. Looks like a dress to me," Jim said. He continued tracing the outline of the belt with Claire's hand. "See? One, two, three."

Claire tried to concentrate on the stars, but it was hard with Jim's hand holding hers. She hadn't held hands with anyone in a long time. Steven wasn't the hand holding type, but Jim had always been. She'd always liked that, too. Finally, Claire saw the three stars that made up the belt, then the rest of the dress came into focus along with the bow and arrow.

"I see it," she said. "I actually see all of it." Their hands dropped to the sand between them, but Jim still held hers inside his.

"You were always so good at finding the constellations," Claire said. "You're a details person. You can pick out the smallest detail in anything."

"You don't have to be a details person to see how beautiful this sky is," Jim said.

Claire sighed. "Yes. It's wonderful. And the sound of the

waves makes it perfect. Just being on this island has been amazing. We couldn't have picked a place more special than here for Mandy's wedding."

Jim lifted himself on his elbow and looked down at Claire. "You look beautiful tonight," he said.

Claire smiled up at him. "That's because I look my best in the dark," she said, giggling. She knew the alcohol she'd drunk was making her silly since she rarely giggled, but she didn't care. She was having fun.

Jim shook his head. "No. You looked beautiful all night, even in the light."

"You're just being silly now," Claire said, looking up into his eyes, but she knew he was serious. He looked at her tenderly, his eyes dark with passion. She'd seen that look so many times before. It was familiar, just like he was. It felt as if they'd been swept back in time to when life was simpler and they'd belonged to each other.

Jim held her gaze with his eyes. Slowly, he lowered his head and gently touched his lips to hers. Claire sighed. She reached up and ran her hand through his thick hair and down to the nape of his neck as he kissed her again, more fervently this time. The gentle ocean breeze caressed their skin as the sound of the waves lulled them. It was a lovely, romantic night. The type of night where it would be so easy to forget the rest of the world and leave everyone else behind.

Claire reached up her other hand and pulled Jim to her. She felt his free hand gently touch her waist and caress its way down to her hip. His kiss was strong and powerful, just as she remembered it. The kind of kiss that could melt all your cares away and leave you wanting more. She hadn't realized just how much she missed his kisses until this very moment.

Jim pulled away for only a second to look down at Claire, and it was just enough to bring her back to reality and nudge him away when he tried to kiss her again.

"I can't," she whispered, his lips just inches from hers. "You're married. I'm practically engaged. We can't."

Jim closed his eyes and sighed, then rolled over onto his back.

Claire sat up, smoothing down her dress and brushing the sand from her back. "We should go back up to the room," she said softly.

Jim nodded. He stood, then reached down and offered his hand to help Claire up. She took his hand and stood. They stood there in the darkness, very close, gazing at each other.

"I'm not going to apologize for kissing you," Jim said. "I like kissing you."

Claire took in a deep breath. "I liked kissing you, too," she admitted. "But as much as I don't give a damn about Diane, I can't let myself be the other woman. I know how much that hurts."

Jim didn't reply. He reached for Claire's hand, and she accepted, then they walked back to their room, hand in hand.

Claire had changed into her night clothes and sat on the bed while Jim went into the bathroom to change. Her phone buzzed and she glanced at it curiously. It was late, and she couldn't imagine who'd be texting her this time of night. She lifted the phone and looked at it, surprised to see that it was from Steven. She opened the text and read it, a frown on her face.

Jim came out of the bathroom as Claire frowned at her phone. "Is something wrong?"

Claire shook her head. "No, no. It's from Steven."

"Then why are you frowning?"

Claire looked up at Jim. "Was I?"

Jim nodded.

"He just wrote to apologize for trying to push me into

selling my house. I knew it wasn't like him to do that. He says he was just so excited that we might be living together soon, and the chance to sell the house had come up and he didn't think about how terrible it sounded. He says he wants to give me all the time I need to decide about his proposal. He doesn't want to rush me if I'm not ready yet." Claire looked up at Jim. "Now you're frowning. Why?"

Jim looked startled. "Oh, I'm sorry. I didn't realize I was."

Claire set the phone down and lay back on the pillows. "Steven really is a nice, considerate person. He's never been pushy about anything at all. I knew there must have been a good reason why he was suddenly trying to convince me to sell my house. I'm glad he apologized, though. He had me worried for a while."

Jim sat down on his cot and it made a loud squawk. Claire chuckled, and he couldn't help but laugh, too. But when he spoke, his tone was serious. "Why Steven?" he asked. "What is it about him that makes you want to be with him?"

Claire looked up into Jim's eyes. She thought it was a bit strange, talking about her boyfriend with her ex-husband. Especially after the kiss they'd shared tonight on the beach. She wavered, not quite sure how to answer.

"It's just a question, Claire," Jim said. "No dark, underlying intentions. I just wonder what you see in him, that's all."

Claire gave him a small smile. "Steven's a good person. He's dedicated, responsible, and secure. And he cares about me. I believe him when he says he does." She gave Jim a sly grin. "I know everyone thinks Steven acts like he has a stick up his ass, but that's not how he really is. Sure, he likes everything to be organized and predictable, but is that so wrong? At least when I'm with him, I know what to expect and he won't just run out on me one day without an explanation."

Jim grimaced. "Ouch."

"I'm sorry," Claire said softly. "But it's the truth. Up until the moment you left me, I thought our marriage would have lasted forever. I felt that secure in our marriage. But I was wrong. I don't want that to ever happen again. Steven would never do that to me. I'm one-hundred percent certain."

Jim looked up at Claire. "Being reliable is good, I agree. But will he ever whisk you off on a romantic island vacation? Or take you parasailing? Or buy you diamond earrings just for the heck of it?" Jim leaned in closer to her and said softly, "Would he ever kiss you in the sand, under a moonlit sky?"

Claire's heart skipped a beat. Jim had always been a romantic, at least in the early years. He'd proposed to her on a spring evening by the lake as the sun set in hues of orange and pink. He'd bought her a lovely gold heart locket the day Mandy was born and put Mandy's picture in it. When they bought their house, he'd insisted on carrying her over the threshold for good luck. Would Steven ever do those things? Probably not. But she'd had a man who did, and he didn't stay.

"No. To be honest, Steven would probably never do those things. But he did buy me a beautiful diamond ring and proposed to me at a nice restaurant. He tries," Claire said. Then she frowned. "Wait a minute. When did you ever buy me diamond earrings?"

Jim laughed. "I will, if you give me a chance to. I'll buy you the biggest diamonds you want, even if I have to use ten credit cards to pay for them."

Claire shook her head. "Now you're just being silly." After a moment, she turned serious. "It's my turn to ask. Why Diane? What did she have that I didn't?" Claire wasn't sure if she wanted to know the answer, but she had to ask.

Jim stopped smiling and his face looked pained. "She didn't have anything on you, Claire. Believe me."

"Then why Diane?"

Jim sighed. "Because she was a young woman who stroked the ego of an old man who didn't appreciate what he already had," he said sadly.

The room grew silent. Claire had no idea how to respond to such a sad remark.

"Let's just go to sleep," she finally said. "Tomorrow's another long day."

Jim nodded and they turned out the lights.

* * *

Jim lay in bed, unable to sleep. His mind was on only one thing, kissing Claire.

He hadn't planned on kissing her. They'd just been lying there, being silly, looking up at the stars, and suddenly he'd had a deep desire to kiss her. And once he had, he hadn't wanted to stop. Every emotion he'd ever felt for Claire in the past had risen to the surface with that single kiss. He missed her. He missed how comfortable their relationship had been, how passionate their lovemaking had been, and just how loving Claire was. The fact that he'd given Claire up for a woman who wasn't even one-tenth the woman Claire was made him sick. Diane had tempted him with her youth at a time he'd been feeling the most down on himself, and he'd been stupid enough to give in to it. It was embarrassing to think he'd given up a gem of a woman for a piece of glass.

Maybe I should tell her. Maybe it's time to tell Claire that Diane and I are no longer together. Jim wondered if that would make a difference to Claire. Would she even consider rekindling their relationship if she knew? That's when it hit Jim hard. He wanted Claire back. No, he needed her back. He loved her. Always had, always will. But how could she possibly ever trust him again after what he'd done to her? Could she ever trust him like she did Steven?

Steven! Even his name left a bad taste in Jim's mouth. How could Claire love such a plain, boring, stiff guy? *He'd never cheat on her, that's why.* But he'd also never love her the way Jim did. He'd known her forever, they shared a child, and he knew everything there was to know about Claire. Jim couldn't make the past go away. He couldn't change the fact that he'd made the biggest mistake of his life by leaving Claire, but he could do everything in his power to let her know he'd love her for the rest of his life. He just had to talk her out of marrying Steven and into loving him again. *Yeah, you idiot. Like that's going to be easy.*

Jim turned in his bed and it responded with an ear-piercing squeak. Jim groaned. But then he heard a small giggle.

"Hey. Are you still awake?" he whispered to Claire.

"Yeah," Claire whispered back.

"Why?" Jim asked.

"Too many thoughts in my head, I guess."

"Thoughts about what?" Jim wanted to know.

"Nothing. Just go to sleep."

Jim turned again and the bed squawked. Claire laughed again.

"That bed really is terrible, isn't it?" she asked, laughing.

"It's hell. And my back is never going to be the same after this," Jim responded.

Silence filled the room. They listened to the soft sound of the ocean through the open patio door. Finally, Claire spoke up. "Just come sleep in my bed," she said. "It's big enough, and we'll both sleep better if we don't have to listen to that damn cot."

Jim sat up, surprised. "Really? Are you sure?"

"Yes," Claire told him. "But it's not an invitation to do

anything else but sleep. You stay on your side, I'll stay on mine. Got it?"

Jim laughed as he got out of the cot and slipped into the king size bed. "Got it. Just like marriage, right?"

Claire turned and hit him on the arm, but she was laughing.

"Hey. No touching. Stay on your own side," Jim said, teasing.

They both settled in on their own side of the bed. After a few minutes, Jim rolled over, kissed Claire on the cheek, then rolled back. "Thanks," he said softly.

Jim fell asleep with a smile on his face.

Chapter Twelve

Jim awoke feeling rested after a night on a real bed. He turned to see if Claire was awake, then realized that she was already in the bathroom, taking a shower. When she came out, she was dressed in a tank top and cotton shorts with her swimsuit on underneath. Her blond hair was dry and loose, tucked behind her ears. Her skin was lightly tanned and she looked young and happy.

"I'll wait for you if you hurry and shower so we can have breakfast," Claire told Jim.

He headed for the bathroom, forming a plan in his head. He decided that today was the day. He'd tell her that he and Diane were getting divorced. Then, he'd try to slowly work his way back into her heart. It might take a long time, but he didn't care how long it took. He needed Claire back in his life, and he was willing to do anything to get her.

Claire had made the bed and was sitting up against the headboard texting on her phone by the time Jim was ready. Jim frowned. He hoped she wasn't texting Steven.

Claire put down her phone when Jim came out. "Ariana says hi."

Jim's brows rose. "Did you tell her we were sharing a room?"

"Of course," Claire told him. "She's my best friend. But I gave her explicit instructions not to tell Steven."

Jim sat on the edge of the bed. "Is Steven the jealous type?"

Claire shrugged. "I don't know, but I don't want to give him a reason to be. There's no reason to hurt his feelings by telling him we're sharing a room. Nothing's happened. We're just roommates."

Jim looked at her seriously. "Have you decided yet if you're going to marry him?"

"No, not yet. I know it's terrible to make him wait so long, but I'm really torn. I'm not sure I ever want to get married again."

Jim decided that this was his opening. "There's something I need to tell you, Claire."

Claire scooted down to the end of the bed and sat next to Jim. "What could be so serious?" she teased.

"The reason Diane didn't come along had nothing to do with feeling uncomfortable with the family. I just made that up because I was embarrassed to tell the truth." Jim took a deep breath and looked into Claire's blue eyes. "Diane and I are getting a divorce. We've been apart for the past six months."

Claire pulled back a little, away from Jim, her brows knitted in a frown. "What?"

"It just didn't work out between us," Jim said, relieved to finally be telling the truth. "It hasn't been working for months. When she told me that she was not coming on this trip for Mandy's wedding, and that she didn't want me to go either, I'd finally had enough. I wasn't going to split up my family for her. She wasn't worth it. Frankly, I realized she wasn't worth it six months after we'd married, but I stuck with her anyway. We just weren't meant to be together."

Claire's frown deepened. "I can't believe this. You're getting divorced?"

Jim nodded. "I'm signing the final papers when I get back from this trip." Jim hadn't known how Claire would react to this news, but he hadn't anticipated her looking pained. He watched as she pulled away even farther from him, then stand and walk to the other end of the room, in front of the patio doors.

"I can't believe this," Claire said again. "You're telling me that after less than four years, you're divorcing the woman you left me for."

"We were never meant to be together," Jim said.

"Oh, really," Claire said, her tone changing from surprised to snide. "So, what you're telling me is that you broke up our marriage of twenty years for a woman who you didn't even stay married to for barely four years."

It was Jim's turn to be surprised. He'd have never guessed this conversation would turn on him this way. "No, Claire, wait a minute," he said, wanting to explain, but she raised her hands as if to ward off his words.

"No. I don't want to hear any more of this," Claire told him. "You know, when you left me, it took me a long time to get over it and forgive you. And even then, I still had trouble seeing you with that woman. But I told myself that maybe, just maybe, we weren't meant to be together and if you were happier with Diane, then I should be happy for you. But now you're telling me that you weren't happy. That you married a woman who you fell out of love with soon afterwards." Claire stopped a moment to take a breath. Tears began to roll down her cheeks. "I just can't believe that our marriage meant so little to you that you'd leave me just to marry a woman who you didn't even love enough to stay married to."

Jim stood and stepped toward Claire. "No, Claire. No. It wasn't like that. Please, listen to me…"

"No. Don't talk to me," Claire said, sorrowfully. "Just leave me alone. I can't even talk to you. Just…leave me alone." Claire ran around Jim and headed out the door and down the stairs.

Jim just stood there in shock. He wanted to follow Claire and beg her forgiveness, but he knew she didn't want to see him right now. He dropped to the bed and stared out the open door.

"Oh, my God," he said, his heart breaking. "What have I done?"

* * *

Claire had run down the stairs and headed to the street in front of the lodge before she realized where she was going. She swiped the tears from her eyes as anger began to replace the heartache she felt. *How could he have left her for a woman he didn't even love? How could he have thrown away their marriage like it meant nothing to him? Had he ever loved me? Or had he only married me because I was pregnant with Mandy?* Questions spun through Claire's mind as she walked briskly downtown. Locals and tourists waved and said hello, and Claire tried to be nice and return their greetings, but it was so hard. Jim had been her first love, the father of her child, and, she had believed, her soul mate. But he'd left her, and now he revealed to her that the woman he'd left her for hadn't even been worth it.

By the time Claire made it to the coffeehouse, she'd walked off some of her initial anger. She wiped her face to make sure the tear stains didn't show, took a deep breath, and went inside to order a coffee and muffin. She'd have breakfast here, and try to work through her anger enough to get through the rest of the day.

Claire sat at the table that was partially hidden from the stairway and hoped that Jim wouldn't follow her here. She wasn't sure what she'd say to him if he did, and she certainly didn't want to make a scene here. She couldn't believe what a fool she'd been, believing that she and Jim could be friends again. Last night, when he'd kissed her, she knew she shouldn't, but it had felt so good. She'd almost wished they hadn't stopped. Now, today, she knew why he'd kissed her. He was no longer with his wife and he thought he could take advantage of Claire's kindness to him. Well, screw him. He was the last man on earth she'd ever be with again.

"Hey, Claire. Mind if I join you?"

Claire turned, startled by Glen's voice. She'd been so engrossed in her own thoughts, she hadn't heard him walk up behind her. "Yes. Of course. Sit down. Do you want something? A coffee?"

Glen sat in the seat across from Claire and shook his head. "I already had breakfast down by the pool this morning. I had a talk with Jim. Are you okay?"

Claire swallowed hard. She didn't want to cry in front of her brother over her ex-husband. "Did he tell you everything?"

"He said he told you he was divorcing Diane and you became angry with him," Glen said.

Claire's lips drew into a thin line. "Can you believe that? His marriage to her didn't even last four years. I can't believe he left me for someone he couldn't even stay married to."

Glen sat back and looked at Claire. "I can believe it," he said.

Claire frowned. "Why?"

"Because he was married to the wrong woman. It's obvious he should have stayed married to you."

Claire's mouth dropped open. "What do you mean?"

Glen leaned forward and folded his hands on the table. "It's always been obvious to me that Jim and you belong together. You were the perfect couple. His leaving you is what never made any sense. He belongs with you, Claire. Always has."

Tears threatened to fill Claire's eyes again. "He didn't want me, Glen. He's the one who left. I was there for him, and he didn't want me. Now, I don't want him. I'll never be able to trust him again."

"Oh, Baby Sister," Glen said, his voice gentle with love. "You can say that all you want, but you know it's not true. You still have feelings for Jim. It's so obvious, and there's nothing you can do about them."

"What are you talking about?" Claire asked angrily. She couldn't believe Glen had said that. "I don't still have feelings for Jim. I'm with Steven now. I was only being nice to Jim for Mandy's sake."

"Oh. Is that what you call it?" Glen asked with a grin.

"You don't know what you're talking about," Claire insisted. "I can barely stand being around Jim. The only reason we've been together this week is because we were stuck sharing a room and everyone else was paired off as couples. We had no choice but to do things together."

"Well, you can tell yourself whatever you want, Claire, but it won't make it true. I've watched you two this week. Your emotions have been all over the place. First you hate him, then you're sharing dessert with him. Now you hate him again. Come on, Claire. The only reason you're mad at him about divorcing Diane is because you still have feelings for him." When Claire started to protest, Glen raised his hand palm up to stop her. "No, you listen. You can't be mad at someone you don't care about. If you really didn't have feelings for Jim, you wouldn't have cared at all that he's getting a divorce. Until you admit it, Baby Sis, you're just going to be miserable."

Claire sat quiet a moment, absorbing what Glen had said. She replayed the week in her head. She'd been nervous about spending a week on an island with Jim and Diane, and then was relieved when Diane hadn't come. She'd been angry when she found out that Jim didn't have a room and they'd have to share, but they'd managed to make it work after all. Then, Jim had coaxed her into having fun, and she had. She knew that if Steven had been here, they would never have enjoyed going bar hopping with the younger group, he'd have never talked her into going up in the lighthouse, and they wouldn't have gone parasailing. Claire had enjoyed all of those things, and it was because of Jim. And now, she was angry with him again. Glen was right. The week had been filled with emotional turmoil between her and Jim. But that didn't mean she still had feelings for him. Did it?

Claire thought back to last night and the kiss on the dunes. It had felt so warm and loving, just like when they'd been married. She'd liked feeling that way again. She loved kissing him. She'd stopped them because at the time, she'd thought he was still married. Would she have stopped at just a kiss if she'd known otherwise?

Claire looked up at Glen, who'd been watching her as she thought it all through. "You're right about the fact that we've gone through a range of emotions since coming here. That was to be expected. Jim and I never had a chance to talk through what had gone wrong with our marriage and why he'd left. It had felt like a death to me, where I never had any closure. And yes, I'm angry because he broke up our marriage for a woman who wasn't worth it. But as far as my having feelings for Jim, I'm not sure what I feel. He can be so nice, and so frustrating, all at the same time."

Glen chuckled. "Nobody ever said life was easy."

Claire made a face at him. "You're no help at all."

Glen turned serious. "Jim told me that Steven proposed marriage to you."

Claire looked surprised. "He wasn't supposed to say anything to anyone about that."

"Are you going to marry him?"

"I don't know. I haven't decided yet," she answered honestly.

"Do you love Steven?"

"What's not to love about Steven? He's kind, thoughtful, and considerate. And he's loyal."

Glen stared hard at Claire. "A dog has all those traits, too. But you didn't answer the question. Do you love him?"

Claire wanted to say yes, she loved him deeply, but she knew it was a lie. She cared about Steven, and she enjoyed his company. But did she love him? She shrugged. "No, not in the way you think of love," she admitted. "But he'd always treat me well and we'd have a wonderful companionship together."

"Is that what you want? Just companionship? For the rest of your life?" Glen asked. "What about passion? What about fun? Don't you want to wake up every morning, excited about what the day held with the person you love? Why would you want to settle?"

"You don't understand," Claire said sadly. "I had all that with Jim, and he took it away. Is it so bad to want someone more stable? More reliable? Maybe lasting love isn't about pounding hearts and passion. Maybe it's about security and companionship."

Glen shook his head. "I can't tell you want to do, but I will tell you to think before you just settle for okay. Because when you have the right person beside you, everything is more than okay. It's amazing."

Claire sat at the table sipping a fresh coffee long after Glen had left. She thought about their conversation. The problem was, she'd already lived with amazing, and she was hurt by it. Maybe settling for just okay wasn't everyone else's idea of perfect, but it sounded pretty good to her.

Claire spent the morning away from the lodge, walking through gift shops and exploring the town. She didn't want to run into Jim yet. She wasn't ready to talk to him. But by early afternoon, she knew she had to return. She and Mandy were meeting with Sandra and Aneese one more time to lock down the details of the wedding tomorrow. And tonight was the groom's dinner, even though there wasn't going to be an actual rehearsal.

Claire decided to walk the beach back to the resort so she could clear her mind. She slipped off her sandals and walked on the packed sand next to the tide. The day was warm and the sky was clear. The water felt cool on her feet. Everything about this place was perfect. The only thing that wasn't perfect about it was her relationship with Jim.

When Claire climbed the steps that led to the bar and pool area of the resort, she wasn't very happy to see Jim sitting on the top step.

"What are you doing here?" Claire asked, all the anger from the morning returning.

"I was waiting for you. I figured you'd come back along the beach and I wanted to catch up with you and talk," Jim said.

Claire walked right past him. "I don't have the time to talk to you now," she told him. "I'm meeting with Mandy in Sandra's office in a few minutes to discuss the wedding plans."

Jim reached out and gently placed his hand on Claire's arm. She stopped and turned to look at him. "Then will you please give me a chance to talk to you after that? We can't have this anger between us, Claire. Please."

Claire stared hard at Jim's hand on her arm until he reluctantly removed it. She looked up at him. "I can't do this now. Maybe not even today, and especially not tomorrow. Just let me be, okay? I need to sort this out by myself first." She turned and walked away.

When Claire arrived at Sandra's office, Mandy was waiting

for her outside. Sandra was on the phone, so Mandy was giving her some privacy until she was finished.

"Where have you been all morning?" Mandy asked Claire. "I was afraid you'd forgotten about our meeting."

Claire took a deep breath and tried to put on a calm exterior. "I had breakfast at the coffeehouse. Glen joined me for a while. Then, I just walked around town and along the beach."

Mandy narrowed her eyes at her mom, studying her. "Is something wrong? Dad seemed really upset this morning and he and Glen were talking seriously for a long time, too."

Claire managed a smile. "Everything is fine, honey. All I want you to do is enjoy today and be rested and relaxed for tomorrow. You're getting married, Mandy. Today and tomorrow is all about you and Craig."

Mandy stopped asking questions, but Claire could tell she didn't believe her.

Sandra waved them into the office and they confirmed the Officiant, flowers, cake, photographer, and the decorations for their outdoor dinner tomorrow night on the patio. The Officiant was a local man on the island who performed all the wedding ceremonies. Sandra assured them he'd be on time. Mandy gave Sandra a CD that she and Craig wanted played as background music during the wedding dinner. Aneese confirmed their dinner menu, the champagne, and when to bring the cake out after dinner. The resort had everything under control, and Mandy and Claire left feeling confident that the wedding and dinner would go smoothly.

Mandy left and went down to her cottage and Claire stood on the patio a minute, watching as two of the lodge workers strung up twinkle lights around the patio for their wedding dinner tomorrow night. It was going to be a lovely wedding and dinner. All she had to do was put up with Jim for tonight and two more days, and then they'd go their separate ways. She'd go home to Steven, and Jim could go on about his life. With that thought in mind, Claire walked upstairs to clean up and dress for dinner.

Chapter Thirteen

Claire managed to shower and dress before Jim came up to the room to change. As he came in, she stepped out without saying a word and met up with Glen, Lisa, and some of the other people from the wedding party who were having drinks by the pool. Tonight, everyone was dressed nicer than they had been all week. The women wore dresses and heels and the men had on dress slacks and shirts with ties. When Janice and Carl came to join the group, she wore a white skirt with a matching jacket and Carl had a light-colored suit on.

Jim was the last person to show up, freshly showered and wearing a pair of stone colored dress pants, a blue shirt and tie, and a tan sports coat. The blue shirt brought out the depth of his blue eyes and his wavy hair fell into place perfectly. He looked handsome and relaxed, and Claire hated the fact that she noticed those details about him.

When the group walked the short distance from the pool to the Harbour View Restaurant, Claire reluctantly slid her arm through Jim's proffered arm. Everyone walked in couples, and it would have looked rude if she'd ignored him.

"You look beautiful tonight," Jim whispered in her ear.

Claire didn't reply. She'd worn a sleeveless, burgundy dress that had a V-neckline, a form-fitting bodice, and a full skirt that billowed out from the waist to just above her knees. Her heels added even more length to her long, shapely legs, and the dress showed off her narrow waist. She hadn't bought the dress to extract compliments from anyone. She'd bought it because it fit her perfectly and it was comfortable.

Aneese had set up two large, round tables that held six each in the private dining room that overlooked the harbor. The tables had been set to match the colors Mandy had chosen for her wedding with cream table cloths and coral napkins. Candles and tropical flowers in short vases decorated the center of each table. It was an elegant setting, and everyone exclaimed how lovely the flowers were as they sat down.

Mandy, Craig, Janice, Carl, Jim, and Claire all sat at one table while the rest of the group sat at the other. They all ordered their meals from the menu. Wine, courtesy of the Fishers, was brought to the table and soon everyone drank and chatted happily. Even Claire had a glass of white wine, although she intended not to drink too much since she was such a lightweight.

"One more day until the wedding," Jim said, smiling over at Mandy and Craig. "Are either of you getting nervous yet?"

Mandy shook her head. "If this had been a big church wedding at home, I'd be scared to death by now, but not here. Having a small, intimate wedding is exactly what I wanted, so no, I'm not nervous."

"What about you, Craig?" Jim asked. "This is your last official night of freedom. How are your nerves holding up?"

Claire narrowed her eyes at Jim, but tried to keep her tone light. "Not everyone thinks of marriage as a life sentence," she said.

Jim turned to Claire, that devilish grin on his face that made him look so charming. "I was just teasing," he said lightheartedly. "It's just that women dream of getting married and men dream of…" he stopped and hesitated a moment.

"Better not finish that sentence, Jim," Glen spoke up from the other table. "Half the people in this room are women."

Everyone laughed.

Claire, though, wasn't going to let him off the hook so easily. "Men dream of what?" she asked, staring hard at Jim. "You started it, so finish that sentence."

There was a long silence in the room as Jim shifted in his seat. Craig spoke up and broke the silence.

"I'm not sure what Jim was going to say," he said, smiling. "But I'm looking forward to a lifetime with Mandy." He turned and kissed his bride-to-be, and everyone clapped.

"Good answer, Craig," Glen said.

Claire sat back, crossed her arms, and glared at Jim.

More wine flowed, and the food arrived. Claire enjoyed her shrimp dinner despite the fact that Jim was only inches away from her. She couldn't believe what he'd said to Craig. Not all marriages ended in divorce. Just all of his marriages.

"Your food looks delicious," Jim said to Claire, apparently trying to make up for his foot-in-mouth error earlier. "Would you like to try some of my steak? It's excellent."

Claire just gave him a sideways glance and didn't respond.

The Fishers had ordered cheesecake with chocolate sauce for desert for everyone in the group. It was heavenly. When everyone was finally full from the delicious meal, Carl stood up with his glass of wine to give a toast.

"I would like to toast Mandy and Craig and their upcoming nuptials," he said. "Mandy, Janice and I are so happy to have you join our family, and we wish you and Craig a long and happy marriage."

Glasses were raised and clinked.

Jim cleared his throat and stood. "I'd also like to add to Carl's toast," he said, looking around the room. "I want to thank all of you for coming to celebrate Mandy and Craig's wedding with us. It's been an amazing week, and tomorrow will be a beautiful celebration." He turned to Mandy. "I love you,

Mandy, and I know that Craig is an extraordinary person. He'd have to be for you to choose to share your life with him. I'm sure Claire joins me in saying we wish you two a lifetime of love and happiness."

Everyone clinked glasses again and cheered. Mandy hugged her father and thanked him for the heartfelt toast. Tears filled Claire's eyes. It had been a lovely toast from the heart, and she was grateful he'd included her.

"That was beautiful," Claire whispered to him. "Thank you."

Jim smiled. "I meant every word of it."

Aneese came in and suggested they move the party to the outdoor patio. She and a waitress helped the group outside with their drinks. The patio was lit up with the twinkle lights the crew had strung up earlier. Palm trees were decorated with lights, and lights were strung above the patio like a canopy of glitter. The couples created a circle of chairs around the small tables and it felt cozy and intimate.

The conversation and drinking continued, and Claire accepted another glass of white wine. She talked with Janice and Carl for a while, thanking them for hosting such a charming groom's dinner. The night was warm and breezy and the sound of the ocean waves carried to them on the wind from the other side of the lodge. The lighthouse shone bright across the harbor. They couldn't have asked for a more beautiful night to celebrate.

The younger guys were getting a tipsy and suggested stealing the groom to go to the bar downtown for an impromptu bachelor party. Mandy glared at them and shook her head. "There is no way he's showing up tomorrow for our wedding with a hangover," she warned them. Everyone laughed and the men decided it was best to stick around and have one more drink here, instead.

As it grew late, couples began to say their goodnights. Glen and Lisa left to go back to their cottage, and Mark and Kaylie went up to their room. The Fishers also said goodnight and headed upstairs. The ones who stayed behind were still laughing and joking, telling stories from the past, and having a good time.

Claire sat beside Jim in the circle, listening to the younger couples as they shared stories. Mandy and Craig were curled up together on a loveseat, laughing with their friends. Claire set her empty glass down on the table in front of her, and started to stand to say goodnight. Jim touched her arm to stop her.

"Let me pour you one more glass," he said, lifting the bottle of wine.

Claire shook her head. "No. I've had enough."

"Come on, Claire. Just a little more," he urged. He tipped the bottle over her glass to pour.

"I said no," Claire insisted a little louder. When Jim started pouring wine into her glass anyway, she grew angry. "Don't you ever listen to anyone? I said no." She reached over to push the bottle away from the glass, but she hit it too hard. The wine bottle and the glass went flying and landed with a crash on the patio pavement. Wine sprayed and glass shattered everywhere. Everyone in the group stopped talking and stared.

Claire's mouth dropped open and Jim looked up at her in surprise.

Mandy was the first one to find her voice. "What is wrong with you two?" she asked angrily. "You're acting like children. One minute you're fighting, the next you're friends, and then you're fighting again. Why can't you just get along? It's only been a few days. Is that too much to ask? For my parents to at least act like they like each other?" Mandy stood and Craig did also.

"Oh, honey, I'm so sorry," Claire said, stepping around the

table to stand beside Mandy. "I didn't mean for that to happen. It was an accident."

"I don't care about the wine," Mandy exclaimed. "I just want you two to stop fighting." Mandy looked from her mom to her dad. "Tomorrow is my wedding day. Can you two please just get through it without fighting?"

Seeing Mandy so upset, Claire was on the brink of tears.

"Of course we can, dear," Jim said softly to Mandy. "Tomorrow will be perfect. I promise, there will be no fighting."

Mandy walked away with Craig, and the others in the group all said a quiet goodnight and left also. One of the busboys from inside the bar came out to sweep up the glass on the ground, and Jim apologized for the mess and gave him a hefty tip. Claire just stood there, paralyzed, embarrassed by what had happened.

Jim came up beside her. "I'm sorry I made you angry. It wasn't my intention."

Claire turned to him, tears streaming down her face.

Jim's eyes grew concerned. "Everything's going to be okay, Claire. Please, don't cry."

Without a word, Claire ran from the patio, through the breezeway, and down the walkway to the deserted pool area. She discarded her heels and ran down the steps to the beach, dropping onto her knees in the sand in tears.

Jim followed her and found her crying on the beach. The tide had come in and the sand around them was wet. He fell down on his knees beside Claire.

"Please don't cry. Please. Tell me what you want me to do, and I'll do it. I just can't bear to see you cry," Jim pleaded.

Claire lifted her head and looked mournfully at Jim. "Did you ever love me? Ever? Or was our marriage always a lie?"

Jim pulled back, stunned. He hadn't expected to be hit

with a question like this. "Of course, I loved you," he said tenderly. "How can you ask such a question?"

Claire locked eyes with him. "Tell me the truth, Jim. Please, just tell me the truth. If I hadn't been pregnant with Mandy, would you have ever married me?"

Jim stared at Claire in utter shock. He took a breath, but no words came out.

Claire dropped her head in her hands and wept. All those years they were married she had believed that Jim loved her, but she'd been wrong. How could she not have known?

The ocean breeze whipped around them as the damp sand seeped through their clothes. Claire shivered as she cried. Jim slipped his jacket around her shoulders, helped her up, and led her to the wooden stairs. She sat, pulling his jacket tightly around her.

"Claire, dear, you didn't give me a chance to answer your question. Look at me. Please. Look at me."

Claire slowly raised her head and looked at Jim through tear filled eyes.

"Six months before you found out you were pregnant, we were pregnant, I had purchased your engagement ring. I had planned on giving it to you that summer. I figured since I was graduating that spring and you had another year of college left, we could be engaged for a year and then marry after you graduated. I had it all planned out," Jim said tenderly.

Claire wiped her eyes with her hand and sniffed. "You did?" she asked.

Jim nodded. "I loved you, Claire. I wanted to spend the rest of my life with you. It didn't matter that we ended up getting married earlier than I'd planned. I wanted to marry you. I wanted Mandy." Jim brushed a stray strand of hair out of Claire's eyes and behind her ear. He looked at her tenderly. "You and Mandy are the best things that ever happened to me."

"Then why?" Claire asked sorrowfully. "Why was it so easy for you to leave me?"

Jim's shoulders slouched and he dropped his head, shaking it slowly. "I don't have a good answer for you, Claire. I was stupid. I was confused. I was a man looking for his youth again. No excuse will be a good enough reason, because I was wrong in leaving you. Believe me, if I had it to do all over again, I'd chose you in a heartbeat. I'm sorry, Claire. I'll say it a thousand times if I have to in order to convince you. I'm sorry."

Claire wiped her eyes again and pushed her hair away from her face. She looked over at Jim. "Then why did you say that stupid thing at dinner tonight about women wanting to get married, but men didn't? It was a terrible thing to say the night before Mandy's wedding. And you made me feel like you never really wanted to marry me."

"Yeah. It was a stupid thing to say," Jim said regretfully. "I was only kidding, like men do about marriage. I shouldn't have, though. I hope Mandy knew I was kidding."

"It wasn't funny," Claire said.

"No, it wasn't," Jim agreed. He looked at Claire seriously. "But it was not directed at you. Believe me when I say that. I loved being married to you."

"Just not enough to stay," Claire said softly.

Jim sighed. "I'm sorry, Claire. Tell me what I can do to make you believe how sorry I am."

It was Claire's turn to sigh. "I'm tired of arguing. I'm tired of being angry, and I'm tired of apologies. Maybe we can just let it go for the rest of the trip. Do what Mandy said. Just get along." Claire gave Jim a small smile. "I liked it better when we were getting along. It was more fun."

Jim smiled back. "Me, too. We'll just enjoy the next two days and throw all the negativity to the wind. Sound like a plan?"

"Yes. It sounds like a good plan," Claire agreed.

Jim stood and offered Claire his hand. She took it, and he pulled her up. They walked side by side up the wooden stairs to the pool area where Claire retrieved her shoes, then walked the rest of the way to their room.

The entire lodge was quiet, bedded down for the night. Few lights were still on, and even the twinkle lights on the patio had been turned off. They seemed to be the only two people still awake on the entire island.

As Jim opened the door, Claire spoke up. "You realize you aren't completely off the hook yet, right?"

"Yep."

Claire grinned. "And you're back to sleeping on your cot again."

"Yep. Kind of figured that, too."

They went to bed that night in their appointed beds, exhausted from the long day and emotional night. Claire lay awake only for a short time, her mind replaying everything Jim had said to her. She fell asleep, no longer angry and resentful, but instead feeling at peace with their truce and hoping they could just let go of the hurt between them once and for all.

Chapter Fourteen

Claire awoke the next morning feeling refreshed. The sun shone through the patio door and the sky was a clear baby blue with white, puffy clouds. This was the day. It was her daughter's wedding day.

She slipped out of bed and looked over at the cot. Jim lay on his side, facing her, sleeping. His hair was mussed, but he still looked damned handsome. He always had with his chiseled features and deep blue eyes. And he had lashes any woman would kill for. Claire sighed. It had always been hard being mad at him for very long, because he was just too cute for his own good.

Quietly, she took out a T-shirt and shorts from her suitcase and headed to the bathroom to shower. She was going to have breakfast, then be off to Mandy's cottage to help her get ready for the wedding.

When Claire came out of the bathroom, Jim was already awake and sitting on her bed, looking at his phone. He looked up at Claire and smiled. "Good morning."

"Good morning," she replied. "Sleep well?"

"Don't even ask," Jim said, chuckling. "Today's the big day. Tell me what you need me to do and I'll do it."

"Well, if you want to join me for breakfast, you'll have to get ready soon. I have to be at Mandy's cottage by one o'clock to help her get ready, and so I can get dressed, too.

"Aye, Aye, Captain," Jim said, saluting her. He got up and

went into the bathroom.

Claire laughed at his silliness. She started packing a small bag with the things she'd need to get ready for the wedding this afternoon. She hung her dress on the closet door so she wouldn't forget it. She wanted to be calm and organized about everything, because there was so much to remember.

After getting everything ready, Claire went out to sit on the patio and enjoy the ocean view. She wanted to take this moment to relax and prepare for the day ahead. Even though she'd known this day was coming, she still had to face the fact that her only daughter, her only child, was getting married. Marriage wasn't the same thing as dating someone. It wasn't the same as living with someone. Marriage meant they'd make a commitment to one another which would, hopefully, last throughout their lives.

As Claire sat there reflecting, her phone buzzed on the nightstand. She went inside and looked at it. Steven's name popped up. Claire sighed. Walking outside again onto the patio, she answered the phone. "Hello, Steven."

"Hi, Claire. I know you're going to be busy today and that these phone calls cost a fortune but I just had to call and wish Mandy and Craig all the best on their wedding day."

Claire smiled. Steven was always so thoughtful. "That's very sweet of you, Steven. I'll tell them that you sent them your congratulations."

"Did you get my text? I'm so sorry that I pushed you about the house," Steven said, sounding remorseful.

"Yes, I did get your text and I appreciate the apology. Thank you for understanding."

"Well, we can talk more about it when you get back. Only two more days and you'll be coming home. I'm looking forward to it," Steven said cheerfully.

Claire looked out at the beautiful aqua-blue ocean in the

distance, the waves breaking softly on the beach in a mass of white foam. She looked around her, at the brightly painted buildings, the inviting pool, and the lush greenery that grew everywhere on the island. She turned and looked at the colorful room, and her eyes landed on Jim's cot. She couldn't honestly say she was excited to go home yet.

"Claire, are you still there?" Steven asked.

"Yes, I'm here," Claire said. "I'd better go. There's a lot to do today. I'll see you when I get back."

"Sounds good. Oh, and tell the happy couple that if they are thinking about buying a house after they're married, call me. I have plenty of great starter homes listed right now," Steven said.

Claire frowned. *Was that a sales pitch?*

"Goodbye, Claire. Have a wonderful day."

Claire said goodbye and turned off the phone. She walked back inside the room and sat down on the bed, thinking about their conversation. Steven hadn't said he loved her or missed her. Actually, Steven had never said he loved her, even when he'd proposed to her. All he'd said was that they'd make a great partnership together, and that they would have a wonderful companionship as they grew older. Claire frowned. But what about love? She wanted to be with a man who loved her. She wanted a relationship with passion. Claire couldn't believe she was thinking it, but she wanted a relationship like the one she'd had with Jim, before he left her.

Jim came out of the bathroom and looked over at Claire. "Oh, oh. What did I do now?"

Claire looked up. "What?"

"The frown on your face. And you're biting you lip. You only do that because of something I said or did."

Claire burst out laughing. "You didn't do anything, yet," she said.

Jim dramatically brushed his brow with the back of hand. "Whew. That's good to hear," he joked. "So, who put that frown on your face?"

Claire decided not to let her own worries tarnish this special day. "It's nothing," she said. "Don't worry about it. Let's go down and have breakfast. We have a long day ahead of us."

* * *

Claire was right, it was a long, busy day. At breakfast, some of the wedding party asked what time they should be ready and where they should wait. Claire advised them to meet down by the pool until a few minutes before the wedding started, then go wait by the arch. Kaylie had already eaten breakfast and had gone to Mandy's cottage. Craig was spending the day with his parents and getting dressed in their room.

Sandra met up with Claire after breakfast and informed her that the photographer had arrived and would meet them at the wedding spot near the beach a half hour before the ceremony. She also said the florist had delivered the flowers to Mandy's cottage and was decorating the arch as that very moment. Aneese stopped Claire on her way up to the room to say the cake had arrived and was in the restaurant refrigerator. Claire's mind was in a whirl as she grabbed her bag and dress to go to the cottage.

"What time do you want me to be ready and at the cottage?" Jim asked her before she left the room.

"Fifteen minutes before the ceremony should be good enough. I'll send Kaylie out with all the men's flowers so you can put them on ahead of time. Would you keep your eyes open for the Officiant and the photographer, too?"

Jim nodded. "You're so good at all of this," he said. "Let

me know if there is anything else I can help you with."

Claire stood there with her bag in one hand and her dress folded over her other arm. She looked at Jim, and it all hit her suddenly. Her eyes filled with tears.

Jim walked over to stand directly in front of her. "What's the matter? You were so happy a second ago."

Claire set down the bag and laid the dress on the bed so she could wipe her eyes. "This is it, Jim," she said. "Our little girl is getting married today."

"Oh, sweetie," Jim said, folding Claire into his arms. He held her tight.

Claire tried hard not to cry, but it was a battle she was losing.

"I know. It's hard to believe," Jim said soothingly.

They stood there holding each other for a long time. Finally, Claire pulled away, wiping the tears from her eyes. "You think I'm crazy, don't you?"

Jim smiled sweetly and shook his head. "No. I think you're wonderful."

Claire felt a blush rise in her cheeks. The look on Jim's face had been so kind, so endearing, it made her heart swell with affection for him.

"Well, I'd better go," she said, picking up her bag and dress.

Jim followed her to the door. As she stepped outside, he said, "Claire?"

She turned around and looked at him.

Jim hesitated, then smiled. "I'll see you in a little while."

Claire nodded and walked down the stairs. For a moment, she thought he was going to say "I love you." It just seemed like such a natural thing for him to tell her. But he hadn't said it after all. And for some reason that Claire couldn't even fathom, she was disappointed he hadn't.

Claire walked down to the cottage, but detoured first past the spot where the wedding was to take place to see how the arch had turned out. They had originally wanted the wedding down on the beach, but when they realized that the tide would be high at the time of the ceremony, they'd decided to change the location. So the arch was placed at the end of a narrow, brick path that led to the top of the dune that overlooked the beach. The walkway was perfect for Jim to walk Mandy down the aisle, and the palm trees around the arch would add to the backdrop in the wedding photos.

The florist had just finished decorating the white arch with a sheer coral swag and the two sprays of tropical flowers that hung on each side when Claire showed up. It looked beautiful. It was even prettier than Claire had imagined. She thanked the florist for doing such a wonderful job and went to the cottage.

The cottages at the Harbour View Lodge were all painted white and had an aqua-blue trim around the windows and doors. Hurricane shutters that opened out were on all the windows and were also painted aqua-blue. Each cottage had an attached porch that faced the ocean view, a cathedral ceiling, and a small kitchen. Claire knocked on Mandy's cottage door and was ushered into the entryway by a nervous looking Kaylie.

"I'm so glad you're here," Kaylie whispered. "I don't know what to do."

"What do you mean? What's going on?" Claire asked.

Kaylie stood there, looking lovely in her strapless, aquamarine dress. She'd swept her blond hair up off her tan shoulders and her makeup was done nicely. The worried crease between her young eyes was out of place on her beautiful face.

"Mandy's losing it. When I came down here earlier to do her hair, she was fine. Then suddenly, she started panicking and talking like a crazy person. I can't calm her down. You'll have to try," Kaylie said.

Claire couldn't imagine what Mandy was upset about. "I'll see what's going on," she told Kaylie.

When Claire entered the bedroom, Mandy was sitting on the bed with her back to her. Her chin-length chestnut brown hair had been pulled up in an intricate up-do with rhinestone pins holding it in place, and she wore the strapless slip that went under her wedding dress.

Mandy looked up into the dresser mirror at the sound of Claire entering the room, and her reflection revealed a tear-stained face. Claire's heart swelled. She dropped her things on the bed and went to her daughter.

"What's wrong? What happened?" Claire asked, grabbing for Mandy's hands.

Mandy looked up at her mother with red, swollen eyes. "I can't do this. I can't get married," she said sorrowfully.

Claire looked over Mandy's head at Kaylie with her brows raised in question. Kaylie shrugged and mouthed, "I don't know".

Claire sat down on the bed beside Mandy. "What happened? Did you and Craig have a fight?"

Mandy shook her head. "No."

"Then what? Why don't you want to get married?" Claire asked, confused.

Mandy started crying again, and Claire got up and retrieved the box of tissues from the bathroom, handing one to Mandy.

Kaylie came over. "Do you want me to get you something?" she asked Mandy. "A glass of wine, maybe?"

Mandy shook her head and continued crying.

"Why don't you give us a few minutes so we can talk," Claire suggested to Kaylie. "Maybe you could bring the boutonnieres and corsages out to the wedding party."

Kaylie nodded, slipped on her heels, grabbed the flower boxes out of the small refrigerator in the kitchen, and left the cottage.

"Okay, dear," Claire said, wrapping her arm around her daughter. "What's going on? Why are you so upset?"

Mandy grabbed a handful of tissues and blew her nose. She turned to her mom. "I don't know if Craig and I should get married. He's so different from me. He likes everything just so, and I'm more laid back. What if we don't get along? What if we end up divorced?"

"Mandy, honey," Claire said soothingly. "You just have a case of pre-wedding jitters. You two already know everything there is to know about each other. You've been living together for quite some time. It isn't like you don't already know his habits and personality."

"No, Mom, this is real." Mandy said. "Everyone knows that half of all marriages end in divorce. People get married thinking they're going to be happy, yet half of them end up hating each other. What if that happens to me and Craig? Look what happened to you and Dad. You two were happy for twenty years and look at you now. You can't stand each other. That could happen to me and Craig."

Claire sat back, astonished by Mandy's words. Sure, she and Jim had a few problems during this trip, but they'd shared good moments, too. In fact, they'd shared a few intimate moments, but Mandy didn't know about those. Relationships were complicated, whether they were old or new.

"Mandy. You can't compare what happened between your father and me to you and Craig's relationship. Your dad and I had twenty good years together. And we had you. Even though we're no longer together, I don't see it as a big failure. And there's no reason why you should think that you and Craig will end up like us."

Mandy bit her lip and looked up at her mom. "I'm scared, Mom. After seeing what happened to you and Dad, I'm afraid of it happing to me. I never thought of it that much, until this week, and after seeing you two together again. It's so sad that you two are divorced. It makes no sense. Plus, Dad's married to Diane and you're seeing Steven. I never saw you two argue even once when I was growing up. Everything was always perfect. So, if it happened to you, it can happen to me and Craig."

Claire had to admit that Mandy was right, at least about part of it. Claire and Jim had never fought. It had always seemed as if they were on the same page. They'd been happy. Yet, their marriage had fallen apart. Claire understood why it scared Mandy.

"Sweetie, listen to me. You love Craig, right?"

Mandy nodded. "Yes."

"And you've both talked over important things like money, children, and building a future?" Claire asked.

"Yes. We both want the same things."

Claire smiled. "Then that's a good start. No one can predict the future, honey, but from what I see, you two will have a good one. I don't regret my marriage to your father one bit. We were happy. Just be sure to always communicate with each other and don't take each other for granted. If you do that, you should be fine."

Mandy wiped away the last of her tears. "Do you really believe that, Mom?"

"Yes, I do."

Mandy sat there a moment, collecting herself. "Maybe you're right. Maybe I do have a case of pre-wedding jitters. This week has been wonderful, but stressful, too. I think it just got to me."

Claire smiled and nodded.

Mandy looked up and saw her reflection in the mirror and gasped. "Oh, my God. Look at the mess I made of my makeup. I can't go out there looking like this," Mandy said.

"We can fix that," Claire said. "Do you feel better now?"

Mandy nodded. "Yeah, I do. Thanks, Mom."

"Then let's get you ready for your wedding," Claire said.

Chapter Fifteen

At a quarter to five, Jim knocked softly on the cottage door. Kaylie, who'd come back to check on Mandy, answered it and let him in.

"Is she ready?" Jim asked Kaylie.

"Yes. She looks beautiful. I'm going out to wait with the best man. See you in a minute," Kaylie said.

Jim walked into the room and stopped when he saw Mandy standing in the middle of the bedroom. Her dress was fanned out around her and the veil fell over her hair and framed her face. Mandy held a bouquet of orange lilies and pink orchids which stood out in front of all the creamy, white ruffles. She looked like a princess. Or a Hollywood movie star. And when she smiled at him, his heart melted.

"Mandy. Honey. I don't know what to say. You're so beautiful." Jim walked over to Mandy and carefully hugged her so as not to ruin her dress.

"Thanks, Daddy," Mandy said.

"Okay you two, let's get a photo of the bride and her father," Claire said from across the room.

Jim looked over at Claire, surprised that he hadn't noticed her when he came in. He couldn't understand how he could have missed her. She wore a strapless satin dress in sapphire blue with a form-fitting bodice that flared out from the waist and down to just above her knees. The color was striking, and it brought out her brilliant blue eyes. Her sandy blond hair was down, and had been curled into soft waves that touched her shoulders. Around her neck, she wore a gold chain with a solitaire diamond pendent on it. It was the diamond he'd given her for their fifteenth wedding anniversary. Seeing her wearing it made him smile.

"Perfect. Just like that," Claire said as she snapped a picture with Mandy's digital camera. "You both look lovely."

It took Jim a moment to come out of his trance at seeing how beautiful Claire looked. He shook his head to clear it. "Let me take a picture of you and Mandy," he offered.

Claire handed him the camera and went to stand by Mandy. Mother and daughter looked enchanting together, and at that moment, Jim felt like the luckiest man alive.

After he took the picture, Jim handed Claire the camera and smiled down at her. "You look so beautiful," he said softly. "You take my breath away."

Claire actually blushed. "You don't look so shabby yourself," she said. He wore a sand colored suit with a coral tie. The soft color showed off his tan and complimented his chestnut colored hair.

"What, this old thing?" Jim said, giving Claire that rakish grin that drove her crazy.

"Geez, you two. Get a room," Mandy teased.

Jim and Claire laughed.

"It's too late for that. We already have one," Jim said.

Mandy covered her mouth with her hand. "I forgot," she said, giggling.

Jim looked at his watch. "It's about that time," he said to Mandy. "Are you ready?"

Mandy looked over at her mother, then smiled. "Yes. I'm ready," she said. And the three of them walked out the door.

* * *

A CD player had been set up near the arch, and as soon as Glen saw Jim, Claire, and Mandy come around the front of the cottage to the brick walkway, he started the music. Kaylie and Cameron linked arms and walked down the brick path, then separated at the arch to stand on opposite sides. Craig was already standing next to the Officiant at the arch.

As the music played, Mandy walked down the path with her parents on either side of her. All eyes were on Mandy as everyone gasped at how lovely she looked. Claire glanced around and saw Janice and Carl standing on the side nearest to Craig. Glen, Lisa, Angela, and Mark stood on the other side, watching the three of them come down the aisle. Craig looked handsome in his sand colored suit with a white satin tie. The smile on his face told Claire everything she needed to know. He loved Mandy. His love for her reflected brightly in his eyes.

The photographer snapped photos of them from a discrete distance as she and Jim walked the bride down the aisle. Claire smiled. It was easy to do. She was so happy for Mandy.

When the trio finally stopped at the end of the path in front of the arch, the Officiant asked, "Who gives this woman in marriage?"

"We do," Claire and Jim said in unison. Then they each kissed Mandy on the cheek and stepped to the side with the others.

Mandy and Craig stood facing each other with the Officiant in the center.

The Officiant was a tall, elderly man who had performed hundreds of weddings on the island in the years he lived here. He had a kind manner and a strong voice that he used now as he began to speak.

"Today, we are gathered here to join together these two people, Amanda and Craig. These two young people have chosen to vow before God to love and cherish each other.

Marriage should not be entered into lightly. It is not only a union of two people, but of two souls. If you give your hearts to each other today, in front of all who have gathered here, you must do so with the utmost love and sincerity, for this is the most important promise you will ever make."

The Officiant paused, then said, "If there be any person here who does not believe that this man and this woman should be joined in holy matrimony, speak now, or forever hold your peace." After another pause, he asked the couple to join hands. He turned to Craig and said, "Please repeat after me."

"I, Craig Jeremy Fisher, take you, Amanda Lynn Martin, to be my wife, and these things I promise you:

I will be faithful to you and honest with you,

I will respect, trust, help, and care for you,

I will share my life with you,

I will forgive you as we have been forgiven, and I will try with you better to understand ourselves, the world, and God, through the best and the worst of what is to come as long as we live."

Claire listened as first Craig, and then Mandy repeated their vows of marriage. Her eyes filled with tears at the beautiful words they exchanged. The site of them promising to love each other for eternity transported her back in time to her own wedding ceremony with Jim, and her heart felt heavy with sadness that they'd been unable to fulfill the vows that she believed they'd both meant completely the day they were wed.

Claire looked up at Jim standing beside her. She could see he held back tears, too. The fact that he was also so touched by his daughter repeating her vows warmed her heart. Then, Jim looked down at her, and smiled. He reached for her hand and held it. At that moment in time, Claire felt more connected to Jim than she had in years.

Mandy and Craig exchanged rings, and before Claire knew it, the ceremony was over.

"Craig, you may now kiss your bride," the Officiant said with a smile.

Craig and Mandy kissed, and everyone cheered.

Over the next hour, the photographer took photos of the family and of the bride and groom. The sun was just beginning to set on the horizon, giving off a spectacular backdrop of pink and orange sky above the aqua-blue ocean. Once the family shots were done, the photographer led the couple off to take photos in various parts of the resort and on the beach. The rest of the wedding party stood around the pool and waited with glasses of champagne, courtesy of the resort.

Kaylie took photos with her camera of each couple in front of a palm tree by the pool. After she took a few of Jim and Claire, they wandered off down the path with their glasses of champagne and stood in a copse of palm trees, enjoying the beauty of the sunset.

"Did I tell you how beautiful you look?" Jim asked Claire, his blue eyes twinkling.

Claire laughed. "Yes, I believe you have already," she said. "But you can tell me as many times as you like. A woman can't be told that enough."

Jim leaned closer to her. "You are beautiful," he whispered.

Claire smiled and blushed. She didn't know if it was the champagne or Jim's compliment that made her feel warm all over, but she liked the feeling.

Jim drew closer and reached up to touch the diamond pendent lying on Claire's chest. "I'm happy to see you wearing this," he said softly.

Chills tingled up Claire's spine at the touch of his warm fingers on her skin. "It's a beautiful necklace, despite who gave it to me," she said lightly with a wink. She backed away a step, trying hard to squelch the feelings rising inside her.

"It was a beautiful ceremony," Jim said, again moving closer to Claire. "It reminded me of our wedding."

Claire nodded. "Me, too," she whispered.

Jim gently took Claire's champagne glass from her hand and placed it with his own on the stone wall beside them. He bent closer to Claire's ear. "I'm sorry I didn't keep my promises to you," he said softly. "I'd give anything to change everything that's happened over the past few years and be the man you truly deserve."

Claire's breath caught in her throat and her heart beat in her chest. She looked up at Jim as he bent his face to hers. His eyes were serious now, and she knew he'd meant what he'd said. Jim placed his hands on her waist and she felt him gently pull her to him as his cheek touched the side of hers ever so softly. Standing together, hidden in the palm trees and flowering shrubs, it felt as if they were separated from the world in a magical paradise of their own.

Jim pulled back only enough to look down into Claire's eyes. Claire raised her arms and encircled them around his neck. He leaned down and their lips touched.

"Claire? Jim? We're heading over to dinner now." Kaylie's voice came from the other side of the trees, startling Claire and making her release her hold on Jim and take a step back.

"Oh, there you two are," Kaylie said, walking around the corner and finding them in the copse of palm trees. "The photographer is finished and we're going to dinner."

Claire took a deep breath and turned to smile at Kaylie. "Thanks, dear. We're right behind you."

With a sigh, Jim picked up their champagne glasses and followed behind Claire and Kaylie to rejoin the group.

* * *

Jim watched Claire all through dinner wondering if she'd felt the same way he had in that few moments they'd shared hidden in the copse of palm trees. He'd meant every word he'd said. He was truly sorry for hurting her and he wished he could turn back the clock and change it all. Unfortunately, he couldn't change the past, but he could do all that was in his power to let her know how sorry he was and how much he wanted her back in his life.

Today was Mandy and Craig's day, but Jim felt it was also his and Claire's chance to find happiness again. Maybe it had been the vows his daughter and new son-in-law had exchanged, or maybe it was this romantic island that had helped to bring him back to Claire. He wasn't sure. But he knew for certain that leaving Claire had been the biggest mistake of his life. He loved her. He'd always loved her. But did she still love him?

The group was seated outside on the patio where the palm trees and plants around them made the space feel secluded and intimate. The twinkle lights above them and the candles on the tables made the setting even more romantic. The moon and the stars in the sky lit up the night sky and the candy cane striped lighthouse across the bay was aglow with lights. No setting could have been more perfect for a wedding celebration.

Champagne flowed freely and the steak and lobster meal was delicious. Toasts were made at intervals, then someone would tap their glass with their knife and everyone would join in until the happy couple kissed. At one point, Jim glanced over at Claire and she smiled back, her eyes twinkling like the stars. He reached for her hand under the table and held it. She didn't pull away, which made Jim happy.

The cake was served and everyone exclaimed delight over how beautiful it was. The group broke out in applause after Mandy and Craig cut the first slice and fed it to each other. Mandy invited the staff to have a slice of cake and join in on the celebration, which they did with happy smiles.

After everyone had eaten their fill, music began to play from a sound system that had been set up just for the wedding party. As everyone watched, Craig escorted his bride onto a cleared section of the patio and they began waltzing to a romantic old tune. After a while, other couples joined in and soon the area filled with dancers holding each other close and swaying to the music.

Jim turned to Claire and held out his hand. He didn't have to say a word, she accepted it, and they joined everyone else dancing.

"No other wedding or reception could have been more beautiful than this," Jim said quietly to Claire as they moved slowly to the music.

Claire nodded. "Mandy knew what she was doing when she decided on this location. It's been amazing."

Jim grinned at her. "Even though you had to share a room with me?"

Claire laughed. "Yes, even with that. Being stuck together actually helped us. It gave us a chance to talk about what went wrong and air out our feelings. Even if we didn't want to hear what the other had to say," she said with a wink.

Jim looked down at Claire seriously. "Do you think you could ever forgive me for leaving you? Is it at all possible?"

"Oh, Jim." Claire closed her eyes and laid her head on his shoulder. "Let's not think about anything other than this very moment," she said softly.

Jim pulled her closer, enjoying the way her body molded into his. It felt so right. They fit so perfectly together. They always had. In his heart, he wished this night would go on forever.

When the song ended, Jim reluctantly pulled away from Claire. He danced a father-daughter dance with Mandy while

Craig danced with his mother. Claire accepted Carl's invitation to dance and soon everyone was taking turns dancing with each other to the soft, slow music the bridal couple had chosen to play. No hip hop, no rock n' roll, only soothing, romantic music that allowed couples to cuddle up together and give the evening a magical touch.

Jim kept refilling Claire's champagne glass until she shook her head no. "I'll be falling down drunk if I keep drinking like this," she told him, giggling. He liked when she was silly. Claire was such a serious soul that it was nice to see her having fun and relaxing after the emotional week they'd had.

The evening grew late and soon everyone began to melt away into the night. Janice and Carl said goodnight and went off to their room and soon Mandy and Craig also said their goodnights. Mandy came over and hugged both Claire and Jim.

"Thank you for this beautiful day," she told them both. "You made my dream wedding come true."

Craig also thanked Claire and Jim for the entire vacation and wedding. Jim shook his hand and welcomed him into the family and Claire gave him a hug. He was a wonderful young man and they knew he and Mandy would have a good life together.

As everyone left the patio, Jim took Claire's hand. "Come on. Let's not let the night end just yet."

She followed him through the breezeway and down through the pool area to the wooden steps that would take them down to the beach. Claire slipped off her heels and left them at the top of the steps. They walked down to the sand, close to where the water lapped up on shore.

It was a beautiful night with a gentle breeze and the moon and stars lighting up the sky. Without a word, Jim and Claire walked along the water's edge for some time. They were both still feeling exhilarated from the delicious food, champagne, and dancing, so it was nice to unwind down here by the water. After they'd gone a short distance, Jim interrupted the silence.

"Kaylie told me that Mandy was having some sort of a meltdown before the wedding. What happened?" Jim asked.

"Cold feet," Claire answered. "I think the entire week just caught up with her and she panicked. She was afraid..." Claire hesitated.

Jim stopped walking and looked down at Claire. "Afraid of what?"

Claire sighed. "She was afraid that she and Craig might end up like you and me."

Jim's face fell. "But we had twenty good years."

"Yes, we did. Or at least it seemed that way. But then we were divorced. Mandy said that if it could happen to us, even though it had seemed like we were happy, it could happen to anyone."

"What did you tell her?" Jim asked.

"I told her I didn't regret my marriage to you, even though it ended. After all, we were happy for years. And we had Mandy. I wouldn't have changed any of it. I also told her to always communicate with each other and never take each other for granted." Claire looked up into Jim's eyes. "I think that's where we failed. We stopped communicating with each other. We stopped telling each other how we felt. And we took each other for granted."

Jim shook his head. "No, you didn't do anything wrong. It was me."

"No, Jim. That's not entirely true. I just assumed you'd always be there even if I didn't have time to spend with you. I put the shop first, when I should have put our marriage first. We were both to blame for our marriage falling apart. I see that now."

Jim smiled down at Claire. "Well, you must have said all

the right things to Mandy, because she did get married after all."

"I only told her the truth. She's the one who decided she wanted to marry Craig."

Claire looked up and their eyes met. The balmy breeze blew softly against their faces and the ocean waves caressed the sand. Jim reached for her. She didn't resist. He pulled her to him and when their lips touched, Claire sighed.

When they finally parted, Claire's eyes twinkled and she grinned. "Race you," she said and took off running down the strip of beach back toward the hotel.

Jim laughed and took off after her. He caught up to her at the bottom of the stairs, both of them out of breath.

"No fair. You had a head start," he said, laughing and trying to catch his breath.

Claire giggled and they climbed the stairs. She retrieved her shoes and walked barefoot across the compound and up the stairs to their room. Once Jim opened the door, Claire stepped in and fell down on the bed, completely out of breath, laughing.

Jim sat down beside her, laughing, too. The room was dark except for moonlight coming through the patio doors. He slipped off his jacket and loosened his tie, all the while looking down at Claire lying beside him. Tenderly, he reached down and brushed a stray strand of her hair away from her face. She smiled, her eyes warm and inviting. Jim lowered himself to her, his face only inches from hers.

"I want to kiss you," he whispered. "I love kissing you."

Claire reached up and gently touched the side of his face. "I love kissing you, too," she said.

Their lips met, gently at first until their kiss became more fervent. Claire ran her hand through his thick, silky hair at the back of his neck. Their tongues danced with delight. Jim pulled away and sprinkled light kisses down Claire's jaw line, searching for the sweet spot on her neck that had always driven her crazy. Claire's sharp intake of breath told him he'd found it, and he kissed her there, gently pulling with his soft lips.

Claire responded by drawing him closer so he was now on top of her. She nipped at his neck and kissed the base of his throat. Jim moaned with pleasure. Claire reached up and pulled Jim's tie loose and slipped it from his collar, then she began unbuttoning his shirt.

Jim pushed himself off the bed and stood, pulling Claire up to stand in front of him. She continued unbuttoning his shirt, opening it wider with each loose button and leaving kisses on the exposed skin. When she got down to where his shirt was tucked into his pants, she pulled it free. Hungrily, she reached inside his shirt and ran her hands over his taut muscles, moving them around his sides and up his back as she pressed herself against him.

Jim reached around Claire and slowly unzipped the back of her dress. Pulling back, he let the strapless dress fall to the floor. Underneath, Claire wore only a black, strapless bra and lace panties. Jim smiled down at her as his hands explored the smooth skin of her waist.

"You're so beautiful," he said huskily. Reaching up, he unclasped her bra and let if fall to the floor to join the dress. He pulled her to him, savoring the feel of bare skin on skin, her beautiful breasts pushed up against his chest.

Eagerly, Claire ran her hands up and slipped Jim's shirt off. Her hands then found the button on his pants and she undid it, then pulled down the zipper. The pants slid to the floor and Jim stepped out of them. Claire reached down and touched the spot that would drive him crazy. He groaned.

They fell back on the bed, Jim on top of Claire, and kissed with a passion neither had felt in a very long time. Jim dipped his head and pulled one of Claire's nipples with his lips, sucking gently, and was rewarded with a gasp of delight. He then found her other nipple and brought it between his lips. Claire's back arched and her head fell back as she sighed. She reached for him greedily, massaging him where he desired it the most. Soon, they were a tangle of arms and legs, kissing, touching, and bringing each other to the height of pleasure until neither of them could hold back any longer.

"I love you, Claire. I've always loved only you," Jim said softly as he lay above her. Claire's eyes met his and she reached up and pulled him to her so they could finally bring their passion to a sweet release.

Chapter Sixteen

Claire awoke the next morning to the sun streaming through the patio window. She lay on her side, facing the window, and Jim lay behind her, his arm curled protectively around her waist.

Claire sighed and snuggled deeper into his embrace. She fit beside him perfectly, as if they'd been made for each other. A smile played on her lips as she remembered their passion from the night before. It had felt so right. So natural. No other man had ever brought her to such heights. Jim knew her so well after years together, and there was a comfort in that, despite the past few years apart.

As Claire lay in Jim's embrace, she remembered his words from the night before. *I love you, Claire. I've always loved only you.* She wanted to believe his words were true, that he really felt that way about her, still. If she were honest with herself, she still loved him very much, too. Despite his leaving. Despite the divorce. But how could she ever believe completely that he'd never cheat on her again?

Jim shifted in the bed behind her and Claire felt a soft kiss on her shoulder.

"Good morning," he said, pulling her closer.

Claire rolled over in his arms and faced him, smiling. How many times had they awoken just like this over the years? More times than she could remember.

"Good morning," she said.

Jim reached up and brushed Claire's hair away from her face, then lifted his head and kissed the side of her neck. A warm sensation ran down Claire's spine.

"I could stay here all day," Jim said, his breath warm on her neck.

Claire laughed and pulled away, sitting up in bed and pulling the covers up around her. "And miss out on our last day in paradise?"

Jim sat up against the pillows and tugged at her blankets. "I am in paradise," he said, grinning. "Right here with you."

Claire reached out and tenderly brushed the hair from Jim's eyes, across his forehead. Her eyes grew sad.

Jim drew up straighter. "Claire, don't. Please don't. I can see the doubt growing in your eyes," he said gently. "Please don't tell me you regret last night, because I don't regret a moment of it. Everything we did was out of love."

"Oh, Jim," Claire said, sighing, resting her head back against her pillows. "Last night was beautiful, and I don't regret it. But where does it leave us? Nothing has changed. Eventually, we still have to go back to reality."

Jim moved closer to Claire, curling his arms around her under the blankets. "This is reality, Claire. This can be our new reality. I love you. I want to be with you. We're still so good together, last night proved that. I'll do whatever it takes to convince you that I love you."

"Didn't our divorce prove that love isn't always enough?" Claire asked sadly.

"Just give me time, Claire. Please. Give me time to prove to you that I will be loyal to you forever. I made a huge mistake leaving you. I will never make that mistake again, I swear."

Claire bit her lip and looked at him doubtfully. *Can it really be that easy?*

"Let's not overthink this today, okay?" Jim said. "Like you

said last night, let's not think about anything other than this very moment. We have one more beautiful day in paradise, so let's go out and enjoy it. I'm sure everyone else will be hiding out to enjoy their last day here, so let's do that, too. We can spend the day on the beach, tanning, walking, swimming, whatever you want. Okay?"

Claire nodded. "You're right. Let's just enjoy our last day here."

Jim smiled wide. "Good. You shower first and then we'll head over to the coffeehouse for breakfast and go from there."

Claire slipped out of bed, conscious she was completely naked, yet not uncomfortable about it. After all, Jim had seen her this way thousands of time before. She grabbed her clothes from her suitcase and walked to the bathroom, all the while feeling his eyes on her.

"Um, you wouldn't want some company in the shower, would you?" Jim asked.

Claire threw him a sideways glance and shut the door firmly behind her.

"Hey," Jim said. "You can't blame a guy for trying."

Claire's giggle could be heard through the bathroom door.

* * *

Claire and Jim walked hand in hand downtown to the coffeehouse. When they entered the patio, they saw Glen and Lisa sitting at a corner table and went over to say hello.

"Well, don't you two look chummy," Glen said with a wink. "Why don't you join us?"

"Coffee and a muffin?" Jim asked Claire. She nodded. "You sit and relax. I'll go get it."

Claire pulled out a chair and sat next to Lisa. "It's hard to believe it's our last day here," Claire said. "It went by quickly."

"Looks like you and Jim are getting along better," Glen said. "You were dancing awfully close last night."

Lisa hit Glen playfully on the arm. "Stop teasing her." She turned to Claire. "I'm glad you and Jim are getting along. I always liked you two as a couple. You fit well together."

Claire raised her brows. "What makes you both think we're together again?"

Lisa shrugged. "I'm only guessing," she said with a smile. "But to tell you the truth, I'm pulling for you two."

Claire cocked her head and stared at her brother and sister-in-law. She wondered if either of them had ever liked Steven.

"Here we go," Jim said, carrying a tray. "Fresh coffee and homemade blueberry muffins."

Claire smiled at him as he set down the tray and sat beside her. She took a small sip of her coffee. "Hmmm. Heaven in a cup," she said, sighing. Everyone at the table laughed.

"Everything around here is like Heaven," Glen said, finishing up his coffee. "We're all going to miss it here."

Claire nodded agreement. In that moment she realized that tomorrow she'd be going back to reality, back to her old life—her life without Jim. Was that what she wanted?

Glen spoke up. "We ran into Mandy and Craig earlier. They're going to hang out on the beach all day. It sounded like they wanted to be alone." Glen waggled his eyebrows. "I have a feeling everyone will be like that today, bracing themselves for leaving tomorrow. We're going on a bike ride around the island. Do you two want to come along?"

Claire looked over at Jim and saw his answer in his eyes. "Thanks, but we're going to spend the day on the beach, too," Claire told Glen. "Maybe we can catch up with you at dinner time."

"Sounds good. Have a great day," Glen said, and he and Lisa rose and left.

"Did you want to spend the day with Glen and Lisa?" Jim asked after they had left. "I know you don't see him as much as you'd like. I really wouldn't mind."

Claire shook her head. "I want to spend the day with you," she said softly. She was rewarded with one of Jim's fabulous grins.

After they ate, Claire and Jim stopped at the hotel long enough to pick up towels, sunscreen, and some water bottles which they threw in a beach bag. Claire also grabbed her camera. Then they hopped in their golf cart and drove to Land's End Beach on the other side of the island.

They found a spot on the beach close to the sandbars and laid out their towels. The day was perfect, warm with a gentle breeze, and there were hardly any people on the long strip of beach. Far in the distance, they spotted Kaylie and Mark lying in the sun. Down on the other end of the beach a boat had come in and anchored by the shore and a few teenagers swam in the water there. Way out on one of the sandbars, a woman walked around with a bag, gathering something, but Jim and Claire had no idea what.

After applying a heavy layer of sunscreen, Jim followed Claire out onto the sandbar. The sandbars ran far out and at low tide were only about knee deep in the water. There was no surf here and the water was calm and easy to walk through. As they walked along, they saw shells, small fish, and starfish in the crystal-clear water.

After about an hour of navigating the sandbars, they returned to their towels and dried off by lying in the sun. Jim lay on his side, admiring Claire in her bikini. She'd worn shorts and a tank over it when she walked on the sandbar, but she'd finally given in and taken them off to sunbathe.

"What are you staring at?" she asked when she opened her eyes and saw him watching her.

"You. You look amazing. I swear you haven't aged a day since we met in college," Jim said, smiling down at her.

Claire rolled her eyes behind her sunglasses. "Don't be silly. I'm old. You must need glasses."

"Nope, I can see just fine and I'm enjoying the view," he told her. Jim leaned over and kissed her gently. "You taste like salty air and coconut suntan lotion. I love that combination."

Claire laughed and pushed him over so he'd lie on his back. Jim joined in with laughter.

Claire had almost fallen asleep under the warm sunshine when Jim tapped her on the shoulder.

"Hey, we should find some shade. You're already looking a bit toasty," he told her.

"Already?" Claire asked, reluctantly sitting up and taking off her sunglasses to look at her arms. He was right, she was getting red.

"Let's go to the resort bar down at the end of the beach and I'll buy you a beer," Jim suggested.

Claire agreed and they gathered up their things and walked up the stretch of beach to the Last Stop Bar & Grill. They found a table in the corner that faced the water and Jim went up to the bar and ordered two Kaliks, the specialty beer of the Bahamas, and brought them back to the table.

"So, tell me about the boutique," Jim said after they'd settled at their table. "How is it doing?"

Claire smiled. She loved her shop and she enjoyed talking about it. "It's doing amazing. It took those first years to build up, but these past couple of years business has increased despite the economy. Thankfully, the age group of women we cater to generally have money to spend and they spend it on clothes. We keep increasing our stock, but now the store seems to be getting too small to hold it all."

"That's wonderful. Just think of how far you've come in

just ten years. When you started it, it was just a small store and now you're outgrowing it. Do you think you'll need to move to a bigger space?"

Claire shrugged. "That would be nice, but rent is so expensive. Ariana thinks we should extend the store to include a shoe line, but I don't know where we'd put it. She's right, though. Women like convenience, and if we had shoes to go with our outfits, they'd buy them. But for right now, I'm happy to be making a profit and I don't want to go into debt to expand."

"Ariana is great. You're so lucky to have her," Jim said.

Claire nodded. "I agree. I don't know what I'd do without her." She took a sip of her beer. "What about you? How is work?"

Jim sighed. "It's okay. I'm doing fine there, but to tell you the truth, I wouldn't mind a change. I've been working for that company since college and I'm about as high up as I'm going to get. Not that I'm complaining. It's a good job and pays well. It's just not challenging anymore."

"Didn't you just go to the Chicago offices to settle some things?"

"Yeah. My boss sent me there to smooth a few things over. What he really wants is for me to move there and run the office. But I'm not so sure I want to live in Chicago, so far away from family. Of course, it would make life easier not working with Diane any longer. But who knows," he said with a wink. "Maybe we'll be grandparents sometime soon. I don't want to miss that."

Claire laughed. "Well, maybe they should send Diane to Chicago and make everyone happy."

Jim's brows rose. "Actually, that's a good idea." His expression turned serious. "You never really liked her, did you? I mean, except for the obvious reason that I left you for her, you just didn't like her as a person."

"Was I supposed to like her?" Claire asked, amused. "Besides, it's not like you have love in your heart for Steven, either. Apparently, no one cares that much for him, I'm finding out. Glen and Lisa just alluded to that this morning."

"What did they say?" Jim asked.

"Only that they like the idea of you and I getting back together. They seem convinced that we're a couple again."

A devilish grin grew on Jim's face. "I kind of like us as a couple, too." He reached over and curled his arm around Claire's shoulders, drawing her close, then kissed her lightly on the lips.

Claire pulled back, but she was smiling. "I think we have a long way to go before we'd ever be considered a couple again."

Jim looked into Claire's eyes. "I'm not going anywhere. I can wait."

Claire's heart swelled with affection at his words.

"Can I get you two another beer?" A young waitress wearing a skimpy tank top and shorts came up and smiled at Jim.

Jim barely glanced at her. He turned to Claire. "Do you want another?"

Claire shook her head. "No. I'm good."

"No, thanks," Jim said to the waitress, pulling a couple of dollars out of his pocket. "But thanks for asking," he said to her with a wink.

The girl smiled provocatively at Jim, then left them alone.

Claire frowned as she watched the girl walk away. She knew the exchange between the waitress and Jim had been innocent, but his wink, and the girl's smile had left Claire feeling jealous. It was ridiculous, but she couldn't help how she felt.

"Let's head back to the hotel," Claire said, picking up her

bag and pushing away from the table.

Jim looked at her warily. "What? Is something wrong?"

Claire tried to smile. "No. I just want to change before we go to dinner. Maybe we'll catch up with Glen and Lisa, or some of the others."

Jim agreed and they hopped back into the golf cart and headed back to the hotel.

Chapter Seventeen

Claire was quiet during the ride back and several times she felt Jim watching her. She couldn't help how she felt. She didn't want to feel jealous over something so minor, but with their history, how could she not? Yes, Jim was a good-looking man and women had always flirted with him, and before he left her, she'd never worried about it. But now, it irritated her to no end. And it made her wonder if he was really as serious about her as he'd proclaimed. Or, was what happened between them just another game to him? She wasn't sure what the real answer was.

They met up with Glen and Lisa on the patio at the hotel when they arrived.

"How was your day on the beach?" Glen asked. He looked tanned and windblown from his bike ride around the island. And happy. He had his arm casually draped around Lisa's waist. Claire couldn't help but think that theirs was a true marriage built on love.

"It was beautiful and peaceful," Jim said. "How was the bike ride?"

"Long," Glen said, laughing. "But really pretty. We explored all the corners and little niches on the island. I think we even ran into a place where some country singing star lives. It was gated all around and right on the beach. Ah, but to have that kind of money."

"We're going to clean up and go to dinner," Claire said. "Do you two want to join us?"

"Sure," Lisa answered. "We need to shower and change, too. Should we meet you back here in an hour?"

They all agreed and Claire and Jim started to walk to the staircase as Lisa and Glen left through the breezeway. Before they made it to the stairs, Sandra called out to them.

"Claire? Jim? Wait up," the hotel manager said, walking quickly up to them. "I'm glad I caught you. I know it's your last night, but we do have a room open if one of you wants it for tonight. We were so sorry about making a mess of your reservation, and the room is still on us, but if you'd like separate rooms tonight, we have one."

Claire looked over at Jim. He didn't look eager to take Sandra up on the extra room.

"I think we're okay for tonight," Jim said. "But thanks anyway."

Sandra smiled and nodded. "Okay, but if you change your mind, let me know."

They climbed the stairs and entered the cool, air conditioned room. Claire immediately went to her suitcase to pull out clean clothes to change into.

"Is it okay that I didn't take the extra room?" Jim asked.

Claire hesitated.

"Claire?"

"Yes, it's fine. It would be silly for you to change rooms for only one night," Claire said, her tone stilted. As she walked past Jim on the way to the bathroom, he reached out and touched her arm to stop her.

"Claire? What's going on? We were fine at the bar and then suddenly everything changed. Please tell me what happened."

"Nothing's wrong," Claire lied. "I'm just tired, and sad about leaving. That's all." Claire disappeared into the bathroom before Jim could ask her anything else.

Claire showered and dressed, then waited for Jim while he showered. While Jim was still in the bathroom, Claire noticed there was a message waiting for her on her phone. It was from Steven.

Claire sighed. She opened the text and read it. 'Can't wait for you to come home,' the text said. 'I hope you have good news for me when you get back. See you tomorrow night.'

Claire put the phone down, walked out onto the patio, and stared out at the perfect topaz blue water and baby blue sky. Puffy white clouds sauntered by in the breeze. Two children splashed in the pool, and she heard people laughing down by the bar. She was in paradise and yet she felt sad. What was she going to do about Steven? What was she going to do about Jim? Why was life suddenly so complicated?

Jim came up behind her and wrapped his arms around her waist, placing a kiss on her bare shoulder. Claire closed her eyes, remembering last night and how wonderful it had felt to make love with him. But how could she believe he loved her after all they'd been through? A tear escaped her eye and trickled down her cheek.

"I wish we were staying here another week," Jim said softly in her ear. "Maybe I could convince you how much I still love you."

Claire wiped the tear from her cheek and turned. "We should go meet Glen and Lisa," she said, pulling out of his arms and walking to the door. Jim followed her, a slight frown creasing his face.

When they got downstairs, they saw Glen and Lisa talking with Janice and Carl.

"Hey guys," Glen said. "We just ran into Janice and Carl on their way to dinner. I asked them if they'd like to join us."

"Great," Claire said, trying hard to sound cheerful. "What did you two do all day?"

"We just took a walk on the beach and then packed up our luggage for tomorrow," Janice said. "We didn't see the kids all day. I wonder where they're at."

"I'm sure they just wanted a day to themselves before we had to leave," Jim offered.

"Well, I'm hungry. Let's go downtown and eat," Glen said. He took Lisa's hand and led the way down the patio stairs to the street. Janice and Carl followed and Claire and Jim brought up the rear. Jim reached for Claire's hand, and she hesitated for a second before taking his hand in hers. They walked to the Blue Bay Grill and were seated immediately at a table by the water. They ordered drinks, then after perusing the menu, ordered dinner.

As they waited for their food, conversation spread around the table. Claire and Jim sat directly across from Carl and Janice, and Glen and Lisa sat further down the table. Claire felt obligated to be polite and keep the conversation flowing with Janice.

"It's a shame our week here is up," Claire said. "It seemed to just fly by."

Janice nodded. "I'll be happy to get home, though," she said. "This has been fun, but it's always nice to go back to a familiar routine."

"Yes," Carl said, draping his arm around the back of Janice's chair. "It will feel good to get back to normal again. I'm sure I'll have a pile of work waiting for me on my desk and Janice was surely missed at her volunteer jobs."

"Oh, where do you volunteer?" Claire asked.

"At the local food shelf and at our church's clothing store. There's always plenty to do at the clothing store. We receive clothing donations from many of the chain stores and we give it away to people in need," Janice said.

"Janice is very involved in the community," Carl said proudly. "It's always nice to give back to others."

Claire nodded. She hadn't realized that Janice did volunteer work and that impressed her. Claire was also taken by the pride that shone in Carl's eyes when he spoke of Janice's work. They may have seemed stiff and snobby to her earlier in the week, but Claire now saw that they were actually nice people, and they cared deeply for each other, too.

Their food came and everyone enjoyed their meal. The sun was setting, leaving a pinkish hue in the sky behind the lighthouse across the bay. Claire's sadness grew heavier the darker the sky became.

The waitress came over to ask if they needed another drink. Claire noticed she paid particular attention to Jim, smiling down at him with a twinkle in her eyes. He had only smiled back and declined another drink, but their exchange upset Claire. She tried rationalizing the fact that he wasn't wearing a wedding band so other women thought he was single, but that didn't make her feel any better. Jim would always garner attention from pretty women, that was just the way it was. But if she and Jim got back together, would she ever be able to trust him completely?

As Claire sat and listened to the conversation around the table, her mind drifted to Steven. He might not be a passionate man, or someone who'd look for adventure, but she knew he'd also never give her any reason not to trust him. Women didn't flirt with him and he didn't flirt either. He was hardworking, steady, and dependable. Maybe that was all she really needed in a relationship. She'd always feel secure with Steven. But could she live out the rest of her life with a man who didn't bring out the passion in her as Jim did? Distractedly, Claire began twirling her charm bracelet around her wrist.

* * *

Jim was trying to listen to Carl talk about golfing but he was distracted by the faraway look in Claire's eyes. *What was she thinking? Why had she turned from hot to cold so suddenly earlier today?* She looked so beautiful tonight in the yellow sundress that showed off her new tan and with her hair hanging loosely around her shoulders. She'd worn the diamond pendent he'd given her years ago again, and that made him smile. But she was a million miles away, and he wanted desperately to know what she was thinking about.

He watched as she placed her hand over her other wrist and began twirling her charm bracelet. Oh, no. She'd stopped doing that when she was happy for that brief time with him. But now she'd started again. She was worried. But why?

Jim reached for her hand and her eyes looked up at him as if waking from a dream. He smiled, but she only stared at him, looking sad. Gently, she pulled her hand away from his, but she did stop fiddling with her bracelet.

"We should go," Claire said aloud to Jim. Everyone at the table stopped talking and stared at her.

Claire reddened. "I mean, I haven't packed yet, so I should go back and get ready for tomorrow. We leave early on the ferry."

Everyone agreed it was getting late and they should head back to the resort. They paid their bills and then walked back along the quiet road, saying goodnight on the patio before going off to their rooms.

Jim reached for Claire before she made it to the staircase. "Do you want to go down to the beach one last time?" he asked hopefully.

Claire hesitated, looking around her. Jim was sure she was going to say no.

"Claire, please. I don't know what happened earlier or what you were thinking about at dinner, but I see that I'm losing you and I don't understand why," Jim said. "Walk with me on the beach one last time. Please."

Claire finally nodded and they walked through the breezeway and down past the pool and bar. There were a few people left sitting around the bar enjoying tropical drinks before it closed for the night. Claire slipped off her heels and left them in a lounge chair, then they walked down the wooden steps to the sand below.

They strolled along the strip of wet sand quietly, side by side, as the moon shone down on them. Claire didn't say a word and Jim wasn't sure what to say. Tonight should have been romantic and intimate, with them sharing a moonlight walk on the beach. It should have been perfect. But instead, Claire seemed a million miles away. Jim was confused as to why Claire was pulling away from him.

After a time, Claire stopped walking. "We should go back," she said softly. "I should pack for tomorrow."

Jim placed his hands on both of Claire's arms and turned her to face him. Even under the night sky, he saw that her eyes looked sad. "Claire. Tell me what happened. Let me fix it. I want to feel close to you like I did last night and this morning. How can we get back to that?"

Claire stepped away from Jim's touch and looked down at the sand. "We go home tomorrow, back to our real lives," Claire told him. "This was amazing, but it's not real. It was just something that happens when two people are thrown together in paradise."

"Not real?" Jim asked, frustrated. "How can you say this isn't real? Claire?" He reached under her chin and gently tilted her face up so he could look into her eyes. "This is my reality. Tomorrow, I'm going home to cut ties with my old life, and more than anything else in this world, I want to make a new life with you."

Claire shook her head. "No. You think you want that right now, but when we get home, you'll realize that this is all wrong. You left me, remember? There was obviously something missing between us that made you leave. What makes you think it will work a second time around?"

"Give me a chance to prove it will work. Please, Claire. Give me time to prove to you that I love you and will make you happy again." Jim's eyes pleaded with her. "I can't prove it to you in a day, or even a week, but I can over time. Please give me that time."

Claire's eyes filled with tears. She shook her head. "I want to go back to the room," she whispered, and she turned and walked away. Jim followed.

"Claire?"

"No. I want to go back. I can't do this anymore. I just can't." Her steps grew quicker as she walked on the wet sand.

Jim sighed and followed behind her.

When they were back in their room, Claire went to work organizing her things and repacking her suitcase. Jim watched her as she carefully refolded her clothes and fit everything neatly into place. His mind was a jumbled mess, he couldn't even begin to think about packing up his bag right now. But he knew that to Claire, this was therapy. Every perfect fold, every well-placed piece of clothing made her feel more in control of her life. When they were married, every time she was upset the house was cleaned and organized to perfection. And now, once again, he watched the process.

He sat in the chair by the window, racking his brain for anything he may have said or done today that might have upset Claire. But for the life on him, he just couldn't think of anything. All he knew for certain was he didn't want to lose Claire again, and he had to try harder to make her understood how he felt.

Jim stood, walked across the small space, and took Claire in his arms, turning her to face him. Startled, Claire looked up at him with big, round eyes. Jim pulled her close, feeling her warmth against him. He breathed in her scent, her perfume, her shampoo, all of it. He wanted to remember everything about her at this very moment in time. How she looked, how she felt, how she smelled, everything, because he was afraid that this might be the last time he ever held her again.

"Tell me you don't love me, Claire, and I'll never bother you again. Tell me that last night meant nothing to you. Tell me that there is no way you could ever love me again. Say you don't love me, and I'll let you go," Jim said softly into her ear.

Claire's body relaxed in his hold, and he felt hot tears fall on his shoulder. Jim hugged her tighter, not wanting to let go.

"You do love me. I know you do," Jim said adamantly. "Last night would never have happened if you didn't love me."

Claire pulled away and wiped the tears from her eyes. "Yes. I love you," she said hoarsely. "Of course, I love you. I've loved you since college. I loved you throughout our twenty years of marriage. But love isn't always enough, Jim. Didn't we find that to be true the first time around? The fact that I loved you didn't keep you from leaving me."

Frustrated, Jim stepped away from Claire. He walked back to the chair, and then turned and walked back up to Claire. "I've told you over and over how sorry I am. I made a huge mistake at a time when I was most vulnerable. If I could take it all back, I would. Claire, I'll do whatever it takes for the rest of my life to prove to you that I'll never leave you again. Please believe me."

"Oh, Jim," Claire said, sighing, dropping to sit on the bed. "Don't you see? It can never be like it was, ever again. I don't know if I'll ever be able to get over the fact that you cheated on me and then left me. And if I don't trust you, how can I ever feel secure in our life together?"

Jim sat beside her and took one hand in his. "You have to at least give me a chance to prove I can be trusted," he said.

Claire shook her head. "It will always be hanging over our heads. Like today. When the waitress at the bar was flirting with you, it felt like a knife being twisted in my heart. And then again at dinner, the waitress was looking at you in a way that suggested she was interested and I felt that pain again. You're a good-looking man, and you're friendly and open. Women respond to that. And those are attributes that I love about you, too. But I don't want to live my life wondering if the next woman who smiles at you might be the woman you leave me for."

Jim's mouth dropped open in surprise. He'd barely even noticed the women Claire was talking about. "Is that why you were upset this afternoon? Because a waitress flirted with me? Claire, it's not my fault if a woman flirts with me. How can that upset you? Did I flirt back?"

Claire gave him a small, wan smile. "Yes, you kind of did, but I'm sure you're not even aware that you did it. You've always flirted a little, that's just part of who you are. It never bothered me before, because I felt safe in our marriage. But now, it hurts."

"Then I won't do it anymore. Hit me every time you see me flirt. Kick me under the table. Pull my hair, whatever it takes. I'll stop doing it then. But don't walk away from me because of it. Give me a chance."

Claire shook her head slowly. She stood, walked over to her open suitcase, and stared at it a moment. With her back turned to Jim, she spoke. "I'm going home tomorrow and I'm going to tell Steven that I will marry him. He's a good man. He'll always be dependable, and I'll feel secure with him. I'll never have to worry that he'll leave me. We'll have a good life."

Jim couldn't believe his ears. He stared at Claire's back, all the while wondering if he was hearing her correctly.

"Claire. No. Don't," was all he was able to say.

Claire turned to face him. "I'm sorry, Jim. But it's the right choice."

Jim stood and walked back toward his suitcase. His heart pounded in his chest. He loved Claire. He couldn't let her make the biggest mistake of her life. He turned and faced her. "Do you love Steven, Claire? Just tell me, do you love him? Will he make you feel loved? Will he bring out the passion in you that I do? Do you love him like you love me?"

Claire's shoulders sagged and tears spilled from her eyes. "No. I'll never love him like I do you. Does that make you happy?"

More than anything, Jim wanted to take Claire in his arms and hold her until she stopped crying. But he stood there, glued to the floor only a few feet away from her. His heart was shattering into a million little pieces. "No, it doesn't make me happy," he said quietly. "It makes me sad." Slowly, he began placing all his clothes into his suitcase. He walked into the bathroom, gathered up his things, and dropped them into the suitcase as well.

"It would probably be best if I took Sandra up on that offer of the other room," he said as he zipped up his suitcase. Behind him, he heard Claire take a sharp breath. He turned to see her wiping tears from her eyes. Picking up his suitcase, he walked to the door, then turned to face her one last time.

"I love you, Claire. Whatever you do, please reconsider marrying Steven. Even if you don't want me, please don't marry him. You deserve so much better than he can offer. Maybe even better than I can offer you. You deserve a man who loves you with all his heart. A man who is passionate about you. That man isn't Steven." With that, Jim turned and walked out the door into the starry night.

Claire dropped on the bed, sobbing.

* * *

The next morning, the wedding party quietly stepped onto the ferry that would take them back to the airport, and back to reality.

Chapter Eighteen

One Year Later

Claire sat in front of the mirror in the cottage while Mandy fussed with her hair. She'd grown it longer so it could be put up in a wispy up-do, and since there was no one to do hair on the island, Mandy was in charge of it.

Claire smiled at her reflection. She loved the creamy, satin, knee-length dress she'd chosen to wear and the simple heels that went with it. Her outfit was understated, yet perfect for a second wedding. And the light tan she'd been able to get this week made her skin look radiant.

It was another beautiful Bahamian day. The sun was shining, the temperature was up in the eighties, and the sky was a rich, clear blue. It was a perfect day for a wedding.

"How are you doing, Mom?" Mandy asked as she continued twisting and pinning Claire's hair up at intervals.

"I'm fine," Claire said. "How's the hair coming?"

"It will look perfect," Mandy said. "Just like how we practiced it at home." A final bobby pin was put in place and Mandy announced, "It's done."

Claire twisted this way and that. It looked lovely. She stood up and hugged her daughter. "I love it. Thanks, honey."

Mother and daughter stared in the mirror at each other and smiled. Claire turned to Mandy. "Are you sure you don't mind my getting married here on the same island as you did?"

Mandy rolled her eyes. "I've told you a million times that I don't mind. In fact, it seems fitting. Besides, how can I complain when Craig and I got to come to the Bahamas again for a whole week?" She grinned at Claire, looking so much like her father.

They'd come to the same little island as last year, and stayed at Harbour View Lodge again, except this time Claire had booked a cottage for herself instead of a room. The wedding party was smaller this time, but they'd all had just as much fun lazing around the beaches and enjoying the many restaurants as they had last year. They had enjoyed a wonderful week and now today would be the main event.

Ariana glided into the cottage in a flowing purple dress that made her deeply tanned skin glow. "What are you two doing just sitting around here when everyone is ready for you outside?" she asked, giving a wink. "Ah, the bride looks beautiful. I love your hair. Mandy, you did a wonderful job."

Mandy smiled her gratitude at Ariana as she slipped on a pair of heels. She wore a simple aqua-blue dress that highlighted her deep blue eyes. "Well, since I'm the matron of honor, I guess I'd better get out there if everyone is ready," she said. She ran over and gave her mother one last hug. "This is it," she said. Then she looked at Claire seriously. "Are you absolutely sure you want to do this? You? The woman who swore she'd never get married again."

Claire smiled at her daughter. "Yes," she said with certainty. "I'm absolutely sure."

Mandy nodded, then headed out the door to join her husband, Craig, who was acting as the best man in the wedding.

Ariana fussed with Claire's dress, tugging it here and there, then helped Claire clasp her necklace. "Perfect," Ariana proclaimed. "Now, all we need is that brother of yours to come and walk you down the aisle."

Claire reached out and hugged her best friend. "I'm so happy you're here to share this day with me," she said warmly.

"Me, too," Ariana said. "If you hadn't hired Alicia last year, I'd never been able to come along. We're lucky to have her at the boutique. She's a good worker."

Claire nodded. She'd made a lot of changes last year after coming home from Mandy's wedding, and one of them had been hiring another full-time employee so she and Ariana didn't have to work all the time. Claire had learned that working too much damaged relationships, and she didn't want to relive past mistakes. This marriage was going to work.

Just as Mandy had done, Ariana gave Claire a serious look. "Is this what you really want?" Ariana asked her. "Because you can back out at any time."

Claire laughed. "Yes. This is what I want. There'll be no backing out."

Ariana shook her head. "Okay, but don't ever say I didn't try to stop you."

Claire rolled her eyes. She knew her friend was just looking out for her.

"So, Baby Sis, you're really going through with this," Glen's voice rang out as he walked into the cottage. He looked wonderful in a tan suit with a burgundy tie. He'd even had his longish hair trimmed for the occasion.

"Yes, I'm going through with it," Claire told him. "So, if you have any reservations, speak now or forever hold your peace."

Glen laughed. "Naw. If you want to marry him, that's your problem."

"I'm going out there now," Ariana announced. "Give it a minute or two and then you two come out."

Claire watched her friend leave, then looked at her brother.

"So, do you think I'm making a mistake?"

Glen grinned and shook his head. "He's a good guy. I think you'll be fine."

Claire picked up her bouquet of tropical flowers and walked over to Glen, linking arms with him. "Then let's get this show on the road," she said.

As Claire and Glen stepped outside the cottage, soft music filled the air. Mandy and Craig walked the short distance to the palm trees where the Officiant and the groom stood, then separated to stand on either side. Claire and Glen slowly walked up to where Claire's future husband waited.

Claire looked up into the eyes of her groom and smiled. This day had been a long time coming, and she was absolutely sure she was making the right decision to marry the man before her.

Once they made it to the grove of trees, Glen handed Claire to her future husband. They smiled at each other, then turned to face the Officiant, the same older gentleman who'd married Mandy and Craig.

The Officiant started with a short speech about the sanctity of marriage, then went directly into the vows. He asked the couple to face each other and repeat after him.

"Do you, Claire Marie Martin, take this man, James Jerome Martin, to be your lawfully wedded husband?" the Officiant began.

Claire smiled up at Jim. A year ago, she would never have thought this was possible. But now, she was the happiest woman alive. She was marrying the man she'd loved over half of her life. Her college sweetheart. The father of her child.

Last year, after she'd returned home from Mandy's wedding, she'd met with Steven and given him back his ring, explaining that she couldn't marry him. Steven had been shocked, but didn't fight it. She'd guessed that deep inside, he'd known they weren't meant to be together, and she'd wished him well with his life. After the time she'd spent with Jim on the island, she knew she could never truly love Steven. She loved Jim, but she accepted the fact that she could never be with him, either.

Two months after that, Jim had come into the boutique carrying a bouquet of yellow roses and a small gift box. Claire was dumbfounded when she saw him enter.

"What are you doing here?" she asked.

Jim handed her the flowers. "A little birdie told me that you decided not to marry Steven after all," he said. "So, I come bearing gifts."

Claire frowned. "That little birdie wouldn't happen to be a brown-haired girl named Mandy, would it?"

Jim laughed. "I will not reveal my sources," he said, winking over at Ariana who pretended being busy at the other end of the counter.

Claire's mouth had dropped opened in surprise at what her best friend had done. "You little sneak," she said.

Ariana raised her arms in self-defense. "I know what I see, and I saw you needed a little help." Then she bustled away to give them privacy.

"The flowers are beautiful, Jim," Claire told him. "Thank you."

"Here," he said with that rakish grin on his face. "There's more." Jim handed her the small box he'd had in his hand.

Claire looked up at him suspiciously. "What's this?"

"Open it and see for yourself."

Claire set the flowers on the counter and unwrapped the little box. She pulled out the black, velvet jewelry box inside it. Gingerly, she opened the lid. Sitting on the black velvet, two perfect diamond stud earrings sparkled back at her. Claire gasped as she reached for the solitaire diamond pendent she wore around her neck. The necklace Jim had given her for their fifteenth wedding anniversary, which she had worn every day since coming home from the island. The earrings were a perfect match to it.

"They're beautiful," she said.

"I told you I'd buy you diamond earrings if you gave me the chance," Jim said, grinning.

Claire laughed, remembering what he'd said that day on the island. "So, do you really believe you can buy back my love with diamonds?"

Jim walked up to Claire and put his arms around her. "Only if it works," he said, smiling.

"This is crazy," Claire said, looking up into his deep blue eyes.

"Then let's be crazy," Jim said. "I'll do whatever it takes to find a way back into your heart. I'll take you anywhere, I'll buy you anything. I'll take you to the moon and back if it will make you love me again."

"Really?" Claire asked.

Jim nodded. "Really. And you know what I want more than anything?"

Tears began to pool in Claire's eyes. "What?"

"To find a way to make you believe in me again so I can remarry you on what would have been our twenty-fifth wedding anniversary."

Tears dropped down Claire's cheeks. "Oh, Jim. I don't know if we can get back to the way we were."

"Give me a chance, Claire," Jim whispered. "Just give me a chance."

And she had. It wasn't always easy, but over time Jim had proven to her that he was the man she wanted to spend the rest of her life with. And today, she stood in front of him in the summer that they would have celebrated their twenty-fifth wedding anniversary and again promised to love, cherish, and honor him for the rest of her life.

"I do," Claire answered, smiling up at Jim.

"And do you, James Jerome Martin, take this woman, Claire Marie Martin, to be your lawfully wedded wife. To love, cherish, and honor from this day forward, until death do you part?"

"With all my heart, I do," Jim said.

After the exchange of rings, the Officiant smiled broadly. "I now pronounce you husband and wife. Jim, you may kiss your bride."

Claire raised her arms around Jim's neck and he wrapped his arms around her waist. He lowered his lips to hers.

"I love you, Mrs. Martin. Now and forever," Jim whispered.

"I love you, too, Mr. Martin. Forever."

As the palm trees swayed from the gentle ocean breeze, Jim and Claire sealed their vows with a kiss.

###

About the Author

Deanna Lynn Sletten is a bestselling and award-winning author. She writes women's fiction and romance novels that dig deeply into the lives of the characters, giving the reader an in-depth look into their hearts and souls. She has also written one middle-grade novel that takes you on the adventure of a lifetime.

Deanna's women's fiction novel, **Widow, Virgin, Whore,** made the top 100 bestselling books on both Amazon and Barnes & Noble in 2014. Her romance novel, **Memories,** was a semifinalist in The Kindle Book Review's Best Indie Books of 2012. Her novel, **Sara's Promise,** was a semifinalist in The Kindle Book Review's Best Indie Books of 2013 and a finalist in the 2013 National Indie Excellence Book Awards.

Deanna is married and has two grown children. When not writing, she enjoys walking the wooded trails around her northern Minnesota home with her beautiful Australian Shepherd or relaxing in the boat on the lake in the summer.

Deanna loves hearing from her readers. Connect with her on:

Her blog: www.deannalynnsletten.com
Twitter: @DeannaLSletten
Facebook: http://www.facebook.com/DeannaLynnSletten
Goodreads: http://www.goodreads.com/dsletten

If you enjoyed **Destination Wedding,** you might also enjoy
these novels by Deanna Lynn Sletten

Memories
(Romance)

Sara's Promise
(Romance)

Maggie's Turn
(Women's Fiction)

Summer of the Loon
(Women's Fiction)

Widow, Virgin Whore ~ A Novel
(Women's Fiction/Family Drama)

Please enjoy the following excerpt from Deanna's novel

Walking Sam

Chapter One

Ryan Collier awoke in the darkened bedroom to the feel of warm breath hitting his face. He was lying on his side, and even though he tried to look at the clock on the nightstand, something blocked his view.

Then that something licked his face.

"Oh, Sam!" he groaned, rolling over and wiping the slobber off with the back of his hand.

He heard the happy swish of Sam's tail on the hardwood floor.

"Okay, girl. Just give me a minute," Ryan said, closing his eyes. Then the alarm clock came to life, telling him it was time to start another day.

Ryan sighed and rolled over to turn off the blaring beeping and switch on the lamp. At six a.m., it was still dark outside and the sun wouldn't show itself for at least another hour.

Sitting up, Ryan pushed his wavy brown hair out of his eyes. He was in desperate need of a haircut. His wife, Amanda, would have told him he needed a haircut weeks ago, and she would have been right. But she wasn't here to remind him anymore—she hadn't been for nearly three years.

A nudge at his other hand told him to hurry and get up. He smiled down at Sam. "Sorry, girl. I'll feed you in a minute."

Sam only smiled back.

After hitting the bathroom, Ryan walked downstairs with Sam leading the way. He went down the hall to the back door and unlatched Sam's doggie door so she could go outside, then he walked to the kitchen and turned on the light. Two orange-striped tabbies sat on the floor by their placemat, patiently awaiting their breakfast.

"Yeah, guys. Give me a second, okay?"

Ryan started the coffeemaker and then turned to feeding the cats and the dog. He scooped canned food into each of their bowls as all three animals looked up at him expectantly. Seeing Sam, he couldn't help but smile. She was always so happy and had that big silly golden retriever grin on her face.

He put Sam's bowl down on one side of the tiled floor and set down the two for the cats on their placemat. "There you go, Punkin and Spice." He no longer felt silly saying the name Punkin out loud, even though he was a grown man of thirty-eight. His wife had named all the animals and he was used to it. Just like he was used to having a female dog named Sam. Five years ago, when they'd gone to pick out a puppy from the litter of golden retrievers, Amanda had her heart set on naming the dog Sam. But it was a female puppy that had picked her, and Amanda fell in love with her instantly. "What about the name Sam?" he'd asked Amanda.

"We'll call her Samantha. Sam for short," she'd said.

All these years later, he was still explaining to people why they had a female dog named Sam.

It made him smile.

Ryan left the animals to their breakfast and walked from the kitchen through the living room to go upstairs. Passing the oak hutch, he quickly glanced at one of the many framed photos of his wife he had scattered around the house. Brushing his fingertips softly across her lovely face, he sighed, and then ran upstairs to get ready for work.

Thirty minutes later, Ryan was back downstairs, dressed for work. He never wore a full-fledged suit—just dress pants, a button-down shirt, and a tie—but he always looked professional and handsome. He was a little over six feet tall and he kept in good shape by working out at the company gym several nights a week. He'd found that staying late to work out helped make the nights go faster so he had less time at home to think about being alone. After ten blissful years of marriage to his soulmate, it was difficult to come home to an empty house.

He quickly poured a mug of coffee and made toast, eating it standing at the counter. He could have sat at the large island or at the dining room table in the roomy, airy kitchen, but he chose neither. He couldn't even remember the last time he'd taken the time to sit at the table. What was the point?

The sun was making its way up by the time he gathered his coat, briefcase, and gym bag. He poured another cup of coffee into a to-go mug and snapped the lid tight.

"See you guys tonight," Ryan said aloud to the animals. The cats were already sitting on the window seat in the living room, cleaning themselves. Ryan's last glimpse of Sam was of her sitting at attention in the kitchen, watching him as he walked out the side door to the driveway.

The March air was crisp, and snow still lined the driveway where he'd pushed it aside while shoveling. In Minnesota winters dragged on, even as far south as Minneapolis. He walked to this compact SUV and slipped his things into the passenger seat. Then he stood a moment and stared out at the stillness around him. He liked the early morning in his neighborhood before everyone was fully awake and cars started making their way up and down the quiet street. He lived in an older neighborhood in South Minneapolis, about an eight-minute walk from Lake Harriet. It was a post-WWII neighborhood filled mostly with Craftsman-style homes, postage-stamp front lawns, and towering old oaks and maples lining the streets. Each house had a driveway and a one-stall garage in-between the next house. But Ryan didn't use the garage for his car. His wife's Mustang still sat, unused, inside theirs. He hadn't had the heart yet to either drive it, or sell it.

When he and Amanda began searching for a house, she fell in love with the neighborhood's charm. She hadn't wanted one of the new cookie-cutter style houses being built in the newer suburbs. As an interior decorator, she saw potential in the cottage house immediately. She also loved the thought of living in a neighborhood where so many people had planted roots for generations. It felt like home to her.

Ryan glanced over at the For Sale sign on the neighbor's front yard to the right. The Finleys finally gave in after living in the neighborhood for over forty years and moved to Florida full-time this past winter. They had been wonderful neighbors, kind and friendly, and Ryan missed having them next door. He hoped the house would sell soon for their sake. Hopefully, a nice family or elderly couple would move in.

Ryan slid into his car and pulled out of the driveway and onto the street. Noticing that Ruth Davis's newspaper was on her lawn, he parked in front of her house a moment, retrieved it, and then set it close to her door so she could reach it. She got along fine in her wheelchair, but he figured her morning would be better if the paper was easy to retrieve. He got back into his car and headed for the highway.

Ryan's base office was in a high-rise building in downtown Minneapolis just a short distance from the Nicollet Mall. It wasn't too far of a drive if he didn't get stuck in traffic, but he always gave himself at least a thirty-minute leeway in the morning. He'd go to the office, collect his paperwork, then head off to the first of his two appointments. He was a computer systems salesman, and he sold large systems to businesses and hospitals. Today, he was meeting with the board of a grocery store chain about a new computer register system, and in the afternoon, he'd be meeting with the president of a bank to discuss their needs. It was going to be a busy day.

* * *

Kristen Foster walked through the home with the real estate agent, carefully assessing every nook and cranny. It was nine in the morning, and this was the first house of the day. She'd spent the last two months looking for the perfect home in a quiet-yet-affordable neighborhood. So far, she was really liking this one.

"Do you know much about this neighborhood?" Kristen asked as she studied the living room.

"It's a quiet, older neighborhood," Greg Carlton said. "The Finleys lived here for over forty years and raised their family in this house. They've moved to Florida full-time now. There's a nice elderly lady next door who is in a wheelchair, and an older man, a widower, next door. You can't get much quieter than that."

Kristen liked quiet. Her work was stressful, and she wanted to come home to peaceful surroundings. She walked all around the main floor, and then headed upstairs to where the two bedrooms and a bathroom were. "Everything looks so new in here. They must have remodeled recently."

"Oh, yes, they did. Most of it was done in the past five years. The floors are the original oak, but the tile in both bathrooms is new as are the fixtures. The kitchen is completely updated. Their neighbor was an interior decorator, and she helped them fix it up for when they decided to sell."

Kristen nodded as she pushed a loose strand of auburn hair back behind her ear. She was wearing her scrubs and had her thick hair pulled up because she had to go to work at the hospital at noon. She'd squeezed in this morning's showing because the house and the price had been too good to pass up a look at.

She loved the old Craftsman-style homes. Even though the master bedroom walls slanted on each end, it was large and they had added a walk-in closet and small master bath. The dormer window was charming, and there was a large window facing the little fenced-in backyard. She glanced out that window and could see into the neighbor's backyard, too. A golden retriever was sunning itself on the small lawn. Kristen smiled. She loved dogs. *Gabbie would love a picture of this one.*

Everything about this home was charming and Kristen found herself falling in love with it quickly. Finally! She was tired of living in the cramped apartment she'd moved into after her divorce two years before. She was thirty-two years old and had a good job as a pediatric oncology nurse, so it was time she found a permanent home. She'd just been too busy working nights and weekends to actually hunt for one. Now that her work schedule had changed to a five-day workweek with weekends off, she could start picking up the pieces of her life.

They walked out the kitchen back door that led to the driveway and down to the one-stall garage. There was a row of bushes that separated her driveway from the neighbor's. An opening in the bushes showed that these neighbors had passed through to each other's homes often. They inspected the garage and the backyard. Everything looked good. As they walked back up the driveway to the house, Kristen glanced over and saw the dog squeeze through a doggie door and disappear into the house.

"Well, what do you think?" Greg asked. "Does this one suit your needs?"

Kristen glanced around the kitchen once more. She loved the homey feel of it, the big eating area with the large front windows, and the cozy living room with the brick fireplace. The large, outdoor front porch was an added bonus. She could picture herself sitting in a rocker, watching the sunset in the evening. It was perfect.

"I love it. Let's put in an offer," she said, smiling wide.

"Wonderful." Greg stood at the island and wrote up the paperwork for her to sign. Kristen walked around the house again as she waited. The living room held a built-in hutch, and the big front window had a window seat. It was all so lovely and cozy. She couldn't wait to sit in front of a fire after a long day at work and relax. And best of all, summers here would be perfect. She liked that it was only a short walk to Lake Harriet, where she could get her exercise walking by the beautiful lake.

"Just sign here," Greg said as she re-entered the kitchen.

Kristen didn't even hesitate. She knew that no matter how much she'd have to pay, this was the home for her.